Doctor Therne by H. Rider Haggard

Sir Henry Rider Haggard, KBE was born on June 22nd, 1856 at Bradenham in Norfolk, England.

After his education he was pushed towards an Army career but failed the entrance exam. Next Haggard was positioned to work for the British Foreign Office but he seems not to have sat that exam. Using family connections, he was sent to Southern Africa by his father in search of a further opportunity of a career.

Haggard spent six years there before a return to England and marriage. He had begun to write and publish some non-fiction in Africa but it was only after studying Law in the hope it might prove to be the proper career his father wanted for him that Haggard began to write fiction, using his African experiences as the basis.

His first fiction was published in 1885 and the following year King Solomon's Mines was published. It was a phenomenal success. His career was set.

Haggard wrote well and wrote often. He managed to sympathise with the local populations even though they were exploited and manipulated by Europeans intent on amassing fortunes in money, people and resources. His writing career covered the great sprint to Empire of several European powers and both reflects and criticizes these events through his well-loved characters including Allan Quatermain and Ayesha.

In his later years Haggard pursued much in the way social reform as well as standing for Parliament and writing a great many letters to The Times.

Henry Rider Haggard died on May 14th, 1925 at the age of 68. His ashes were buried at Ditchingham Church.

Index of Contents

H. RIDER HAGGARD – A CONCISE BIBLIOGRAPHY

AUTHOR'S NOTE

Some months since the leaders of the Government dismayed their supporters and astonished the world by a sudden surrender to the clamour of the anti-vaccinationists. In the space of a single evening, with a marvellous versatility, they threw to the agitators the ascertained results of generations of the medical faculty, the report of a Royal Commission, what are understood to be their own convictions, and the President of the Local Government Board. After one ineffectual fight the House of Lords answered to the whip, and, under the guise of a "graceful concession," the health of the country was given without appeal into the hand of the "Conscientious Objector."

In his perplexity it has occurred to an observer of these events—as a person who in other lands has seen and learned something of the ravages of smallpox among the unvaccinated—to try to forecast their natural and, in the view of many, their almost certain end. Hence these pages from the life history of the pitiable, but unfortunate Dr. Therne.[*] Absit omen! May the prophecy be falsified! But, on the other hand, it may not. Some who are very competent to judge say that it will not; that, on the contrary, this strange paralysis of "the most powerful ministry of the generation" must result hereafter in much terror, and in the sacrifice of innocent lives.

[*] *It need hardly be explained that Dr. Therne himself is a character convenient to the dramatic purpose of the story, and in no way intended to be taken as a type of anti- vaccinationist medical men, who are, the author believes, as conscientious in principle as they are select in number.*

The importance of the issue to those helpless children from whom the State has thus withdrawn its shield, is this writer's excuse for inviting the public to interest itself in a medical tale. As for the moral, each reader can fashion it to his fancy.

CHAPTER I

THE DILIGENCE

James Therne is not my real name, for why should I publish it to the world? A year or two ago it was famous—or infamous—enough, but in that time many things have happened. There has been a war, a continental revolution, two scandals of world-wide celebrity, one moral and the other financial, and, to come to events that interest me particularly as a doctor, an epidemic of Asiatic plague in Italy and France, and, stranger still, an outbreak of the mediaeval grain sickness, which is believed to have carried off 20,000 people in Russia and German Poland, consequent, I have no doubt, upon the wet season and poor rye harvest in those countries.

These occurrences and others are more than enough to turn the public mind from the recollection of the appalling smallpox epidemic that passed over England last autumn two years, of which the first fury broke upon the city of Dunchester, my native place, that for many years I had the honour to represent in Parliament. The population of Dunchester, it is true, is smaller by over five thousand souls, and many of those who survive are not so good-looking as they were, but the gap is easily filled and pock-marks are not hereditary. Also, such a horror will never happen again, for now the law of compulsory vaccination is strong enough! Only the dead have cause of complaint, those who were cut off from the world and despatched hot-foot whither we see not. Myself I am certain of nothing; I know too much about the brain and body to have much faith in the soul, and I pray to God that I may be right. Ah! there it comes in. If a God, why not the rest, and who shall say there is no God? Somehow it seems to me that more than once in my life I have seen His Finger.

Yet I pray that I am right, for if I am wrong what a welcome awaits me yonder when grief and chloral and that "slight weakness of the heart" have done their work.

Yes—five thousand of them or more in Dunchester alone, and, making every allowance, I suppose that in this one city there were very many of these—young people mostly—who owed their deaths to me, since it was my persuasion, my eloquent arguments, working upon the minds of their prejudiced and credulous elders, that surely, if indirectly, brought their doom upon them. "A doctor is not infallible, he may make mistakes." Quite so, and if a mistake of his should kill a few thousands, why, that is the act of God (or of Fate) working through his blindness. But if it does not happen to have been a mistake, if, for instance, all those dead, should they still live in any place or shape, could say to me, "James Therne, you are the murderer of our bodies, since, for your own ends, you taught us that which you knew not to be the truth."

How then? I ask. So—let them say it if they will. Let all that great cloud of witnesses compass me about, lads and maidens, children and infants, whose bones cumber the churchyards yonder in Dunchester. I defy them, for it is done and cannot be undone. Yet, in their company are two whose eyes I dread to meet: Jane, my daughter, whose life was sacrificed through me, and Ernest Merchison, her lover, who went to seek her in the tomb.

They would not reproach me now, I know, for she was too sweet and loved me too well with all my faults, and, if he proved pitiless in the first torment of his loss, Merchison was a good and honest man, who, understanding my remorse and misery, forgave me before he died. Still, I dread to meet them, who, if that old fable be true and they live, read me for what I am. Yet why should I fear, for all this they knew before they died, and, knowing, could forgive? Surely it is with another vengeance that I must reckon.

Well, after her mother's death my daughter was the only being whom I ever truly loved, and no future mental hell that the imagination can invent would have power to make me suffer more because of her than I have always suffered since the grave closed over her—the virgin martyr sacrificed on the altar of a false prophet and a coward.

I come of a family of doctors. My grandfather, Thomas Therne, whose name still lives in medicine, was a doctor in the neighbourhood of Dunchester, and my father succeeded to his practice and nothing else, for the old gentleman had lived beyond his means. Shortly after my father's marriage he sold this practice and removed into Dunchester, where he soon acquired a considerable reputation as a surgeon, and prospered, until not long after my birth, just as a brilliant career seemed to be opening itself to him, death closed his book for ever. In attending a case of smallpox, about four months before I was born, he contracted the disease, but the attack was not considered serious and he recovered from it quickly. It would seem, however, that it left some constitutional weakness, for a year later he was found to be suffering from tuberculosis of the lungs, and was ordered to a warmer climate.

Selling his Dunchester practice for what it would fetch to his assistant, Dr. Bell, my father came to Madeira—whither, I scarcely know why, I have also drifted now that all is over for me—for here he hoped to be able to earn a living by doctoring the English visitors. This, however, he could not do, since the climate proved no match for his disease, though he lingered for nearly two years, during which time he spent all the money that he had. When he died there was scarcely enough left to pay for his funeral in the little churchyard yonder that I can see from the windows of this quinta. Where he lies exactly I do not know as no record was kept, and the wooden cross, the only monument that my mother could afford to set over him, has long ago rotted away.

Some charitable English people helped my mother to return to England, where we went to live with her mother, who existed on a pension of about 120 pounds a year, in a fishing-village near Brighton. Here I grew up, getting my education—a very good one by the way—at a cheap day school. My mother's wish was that I should become a sailor like her own father, who had been a captain in the Navy, but the necessary money was not forthcoming to put me into the Royal Navy, and my liking for the sea was not strong enough to take me into the merchant service.

From the beginning I wished to be a doctor like my father and grandfather before me, for I knew that I was clever, and I knew also that successful doctors make a great deal of money. Ground down as I had been by poverty from babyhood, already at nineteen years of age I desired money above everything on earth. I saw then, and subsequent experience has only confirmed my views, that the world as it has become under the pressure of high civilisation is a world for the rich. Leaving material comforts and advantages out of the question, what ambition can a man satisfy without money? Take the successful politicians for instance, and it will be found that almost every one of them is rich. This country is too full; there is scant room for the individual. Only intellectual Titans can force their heads above the crowd, and, as a rule, they have not even then the money to take them higher. If I had my life over again—and it is my advice to all young men of ability and ambition—I would leave the old country and settle in America or in one of the great colonies. There, where the conditions are more elastic and the competition is not so cruel, a hard-working man of talent does not need to be endowed with fortune to enable him to rise to the top of the tree.

Well, my desire was to be accomplished, for as it chanced a younger brother of my father, who during his lifetime had never taken any notice of me, died and left me 750 pounds. Seven hundred and fifty pounds! To me at that time it was colossal wealth, for it enabled us to rent some rooms in London, where I entered myself as a medical student at University College.

There is no need for me to dwell upon my college career, but if any one were to take the trouble to consult the old records he would find that it was sufficiently brilliant. I worked hard, and I had a natural, perhaps an hereditary liking, for the work. Medicine always fascinated me. I think it the greatest of the sciences, and from the beginning I was determined that I would be among the greatest of its masters.

At four and twenty, having finished my curriculum with high honours—I was gold medallist of my year in both medicine and surgery—I became house-surgeon to one of the London hospitals. After my term of office was over I remained at the hospital for another year, for I wished to make a practical study of my profession in all its branches before starting a private practice. At the end of this time my mother died while still comparatively young. She had never really recovered from the loss of my father, and, though it was long about it, sorrow sapped her strength at last. Her loss was a shock to me, although in fact we had few tastes in common. To divert my mind, and also because I was somewhat run down and really needed a change, I asked a friend of mine who was a director of a great steamship line running to the

West Indies and Mexico to give me a trip out, offering my medicine services in return for the passage. This he agreed to do with pleasure; moreover, matters were so arranged that I could stop in Mexico for three months and rejoin the vessel on her next homeward trip.

After a very pleasant voyage I reached Vera Cruz. It is a quaint and in some ways a pretty place, with its tall cool-looking houses and narrow streets, not unlike Funchal, only more tropical. Whenever I think of it, however, the first memories that leap to my mind are those of the stench of the open drains and of the scavenger carts going their rounds with the zaphilotes or vultures actually sitting upon them. As it happened, those carts were very necessary then, for a yellow fever epidemic was raging in the place. Having nothing particular to do I stopped there for three weeks to study it, working in the hospitals with the local doctors, for I felt no fear of yellow fever—only one contagious disease terrifies me, and with that I was soon destined to make acquaintance.

At length I arranged to start for the City of Mexico, to which in those days the journey from Vera Cruz was performed by diligence as the railway as not yet finished. At that time Mexico was a wild country. Wars and revolutions innumerable, together with a certain natural leaning that way, had reduced a considerable proportion of its inhabitants to the road, where they earned a precarious living—not by mending it, but by robbing and occasionally cutting the throats of any travellers whom they could catch.

The track from Vera Cruz to Mexico City runs persistently uphill; indeed, I think the one place is 7000 feet above the level of the other. First, there is the hot zone, where the women by the wayside sell you pineapples and cocoanuts; then the temperate zone, where they offer you oranges and bananas; then the cold country, in which you are expected to drink a filthy liquid extracted from aloes called pulque, that in taste and appearance resembles soapy water.

It was somewhere in the temperate zone that we passed a town consisting of fifteen adobe or mud houses and seventeen churches. The excessive religious equipment of this city is accounted for by an almost inaccessible mountain stronghold in the neighbourhood. This stronghold for generations had been occupied by brigands, and it was the time-honoured custom of each chieftain of the band, when he retired on a hard-earned competence, to expiate any regrettable incidents in his career by building a church in the town dedicated to his patron saint and to the memory of those whose souls he had helped to Paradise. This pious and picturesque, if somewhat mediaeval, custom has now come to an end, as I understand that the Mexican Government caused the stronghold to be stormed a good many years ago, and put its occupants, to the number of several hundreds, to the sword.

We were eight in the coach, which was drawn by as many mules—four merchants, two priests, myself and the lady who afterwards became my wife. She was a blue-eyed and fair-haired American from New York. Her name, I soon discovered, was Emma Becker, and her father, who was dead, had been a lawyer. We made friends at once, and before we had jolted ten miles on our journey I learned her story. It seemed that she was an orphan with a very small fortune, and only one near relative, an aunt who had married a Mexican named Gomez, the owner of a fine range or hacienda situated on the border of the highlands, about eighty miles from the City of Mexico. On the death of her father, being like most American girls adventurous and independent, Miss Becker had accepted an invitation from her aunt Gomez and her husband to come and live with them a while. Now, quite alone and unescorted, she was on her way to Mexico City, where she expected to be met by some friends of her uncle.

We started from Vera Cruz about mid-day and slept, or rather passed the night, at a filthy inn alive with every sort of insect pest. Two hours before dawn we were bundled into the diligencia and slowly dragged up a mountain road so steep that, notwithstanding the blows and oaths of the drivers, the mules had to stop every few hundred yards to rest. I remember that at last I fell asleep, my head reposing on the shoulder of a very fat priest, who snored tempestuously, then awoke to pray, then snored again. It was the voice of Miss Becker, who sat opposite to me, that wakened me.

"Forgive me for disturbing you, Dr. Therne," she said, "but you really must look," and she pointed through the window of the coach.

Following her hand I saw a sight which no one who has witnessed it can ever forget: the sun rising on the mighty peak of Orizaba, the Star Mountain, as the old Aztecs named it. Eighteen thousand feet above our heads towered the great volcano, its foot clothed with forests, its cone dusted with snow. The green flanks of the peak and the country beneath them were still wrapped in shadow, but on its white and lofty crest already the lights of dawn were burning. Never have I seen anything more beautiful than this soaring mountain top flaming like some giant torch over a world of darkness; indeed, the unearthly grandeur of the sight amazed and half paralysed my mind.

A lantern swung from the roof of the coach, and, turning my eyes from the mountain, in its light I saw the face of my travelling companion and—fell in love with it. I had seen it before without any such idea entering my mind; then it had been to me only the face of a rather piquante and pretty girl, but with this strange and inconvenient result, the sight of the dawn breaking upon Orizaba seemed to have worked some change in me. At least, if only for an instant, it had pierced the barrier that day by day we build within us to protect ourselves from the attack of the impulses of nature.

In that moment at any rate there was a look upon this girl's countenance and a light shining in her eyes which overcame my caution and swept me out of myself, for I think that she too was under the shadow of the glory which broke upon the crest of Orizaba. In vain did I try to save myself and to struggle back to common-sense, since hitherto the prospect of domestic love had played no part in my scheme of life. It was useless, so I gave it up, and our eyes met.

Neither of us said anything, but from that time forward we knew that we did not wish to be parted any more.

After a while, to relieve a tension of mind which neither of us cared to reveal, we drifted into desultory and indifferent conversation. In the course of our talk Emma told me that her aunt had written to her that if she could leave the coach at Orizaba she would be within fifty miles of the hacienda of La Concepcion, whereas when she reached Mexico City she would still be eighty miles from it. Her aunt had added, however, that this was not practicable at present, why she did not say, and that she must go on to Mexico where some friends would take charge of her until her uncle was able to fetch her.

Presently Emma seemed to fall asleep, at least she shut her eyes. But I could not sleep, and sat there listening to the snores of the fat priest and the strange interminable oaths of the drivers as they thrashed the mules. Opposite to me, tied to the roof of the coach immediately above Emma's head, was a cheap looking-glass, provided, I suppose, for the convenience of passengers when making the toilette of travel. In it I could see myself reflected, so, having nothing better to do, in view of contingencies which of a sudden had become possible, I amused myself by taking count of my personal appearance. On the whole in those days it was not unsatisfactory. In build, I was tall and slight, with thin, nervous hands. My colouring and hair were dark, and I had soft and rather large brown eyes. The best part of my face was my forehead, which was ample, and the worst my mouth, which was somewhat weak. I do not think, however, that any one would have guessed by looking at me as I then appeared at the age of seven and twenty, that I was an exceedingly hard-working man with extraordinary powers of observation and a really retentive memory.

At any rate, I am sure that it was not these qualities which recommended me to Emma Becker, nor, whatever we may have felt under the influences of Orizaba, was it any spiritual affinity. Doctors, I fear, are not great believers in spiritual affinities; they know that such emotions can be accounted for in other ways. Probably Emma was attracted to me because I was dark, and I to her because she was fair. Orizaba and opportunity merely brought out and accentuated these quite natural preferences.

By now the day had broken, and, looking out of the window, I could see that we were travelling along the side of a mountain. Above us the slope was gentle and clothed with sub-tropical trees, while below it became a veritable precipice, in some places absolutely sheer, for the road was cut upon a sort of rocky ledge, although, owing to the vast billows of mist that filled it, nothing could be seen of the gulf beneath.

I was reflecting, I remember, that this would be an ill path to drive with a drunken coachman, when suddenly I saw the off-front mule stumble unaccountably, and, as it fell, heard a shot fired close at hand. Next instant also I saw the driver and his companion spring from the box, and, with a yell of terror, plunge over the edge of the cliff, apparently into the depths below. Then from the narrow compass of that coach arose a perfect pandemonium of sounds, with an under cry of a single word, "Brigands! Brigands!"

The merchants shouted, supplicated their saints, and swore as with trembling hands they tried to conceal loose valuables in their boots and hats; one of the priests too literally howled in his terror, but the other, a man of more dignity, only bowed his head and murmured a prayer. By this time also the mules had tied themselves into a knot and were threatening to overturn the coach, to prevent which our captors, before meddling with us, cut the animals loose with their machetes or swords, and drove them over the brink of the abyss, where, like the drivers, they vanished. Then a dusky-faced ruffian, with a scar on his cheek, came to the door of the diligence and bowing politely beckoned to us to come out. As there were at least a dozen of them and resistance was useless, even if our companions could have found the courage to fight, we obeyed, and were placed before the brigands in a line, our backs being set to the edge of the gulf. I was last but one in the line, and beyond me stood Emma Becker, whose hand I held.

Then the tragedy began. Several of the villains seized the first merchant, and, stopping his cries and protestations with a blow in the mouth, stripped him to the shirt, abstracting notes and gold and everything else of value that they could find in various portions of his attire where he had hidden them, and principally, I remember, from the lining of his vest. When they had done with him, they dragged him away and bundled him roughly into the diligence.

Next to this merchant stood the two priests. Of the first of these the brigands asked a question, to which, with some hesitation, the priest—that man who had shown so much terror—replied in the affirmative, whereon his companion looked at him contemptuously and muttered a Spanish phrase which means "Man without shame." Of him also the same question was asked, in answer to which he shook his head, whereon he was conducted, though without violence or being searched, to the coach, and shut into it with the plundered merchant. Then the thieves went to work with the next victim.

"Dr. Therne," whispered Emma Becker, "you have a pistol, do you not?"

I nodded my head.

"Will you lend it me? You understand?"

"Yes," I answered, "I understand, but I hope that things are not so bad as that."

"They are," she answered with a quiver in her voice. "I have heard about these Mexican brigands. With the exception of that priest and myself they will put all of you into the coach and push it over the precipice."

At her words my heart stood still and a palpable mist gathered before my eyes. When it cleared away my brain seemed to awake to an abnormal activity, as though the knowledge that unless it was used to good effect now it would never be used again were spurring it to action. Rapidly I reviewed the situation and considered every possible method of escape. At first I could think of none; then suddenly I remembered that the driver and his companion, who no doubt knew every inch of the road, had leaped from the coach, apparently over the edge of the precipice. This I felt sure they would not have done had they been going to certain death, since they would have preferred to take their chance of mercy at the hands of the brigands. Moreover, these gentry themselves had driven the mules into the abyss whither those wise animals would never have gone unless there was some foothold for them.

I looked behind me but could discover nothing, for, as is common in Mexico at the hour of dawn, the gulf was absolutely filled with dense vapours. Then I made up my mind that I would risk it and began to shuffle slowly backwards. Already I was near the edge when I remembered Emma Becker and paused to reflect. If I took her with me it would considerably lessen my chances of escape, and at any rate her life was not threatened. But I had not given her the pistol, and at that moment even in my panic there rose before me a vision of her face as I had seen it in the lamplight when she looked up at the glory shining on the crest of Orizaba.

Had it not been for this vision I think it possible that I might have left her. I wish to gloze over nothing; I did not make my own nature, and in these pages I describe it as it was and is without palliation or excuse. I know that this is not the fashion in autobiographies; no one has done it since the time of Pepys, who did not write for publication, and for that very reason my record has its value. I am physically and, perhaps morally also, timid—that is, although I have faced it boldly enough upon occasion, as the reader will learn in the course of my history, I fear the thought of death, and especially of cruel and violent death, such as was near to me at that moment. So much did I fear it then that the mere fact that an acquaintance was in danger and distress would scarcely have sufficed to cause me to sacrifice, or at least to greatly complicate, my own chances of escape in order to promote hers simply because that acquaintance was of the other sex. But Emma had touched a new chord in my nature, and I felt, whether I liked it or not, that whatever I could do for myself I must do for her also. So I shuffled forward again.

"Listen," I whispered, "I have been to look and I do not believe that the cliff is very steep just here. Will you try it with me?"

"Of course," she answered; "I had as soon die of a broken neck as in any other way."

"We must watch our chance then, or they will see us run and shoot. Wait till I give you the signal."

She nodded her head and we waited.

At length, while the fourth and last merchant, who stood next to me, was being dealt with, just as in our despair we were about to throw ourselves into the gulf before them all, fortune gave us our opportunity. This unhappy man, having probably some inkling of the doom which awaited him, broke suddenly from the hands of his captors, and ran at full speed down the road. After him they went pell-mell, every thief of them except one who remained—fortunately for us upon its farther side—on guard by the door of the diligence in which four people, three merchants and a priest, were now imprisoned. With laughs and shouts they hunted their wretched quarry, firing shots as they ran, till at length one of them overtook the man and cut him down with his machete.

"Don't look, but come," I whispered to my companion.

In another instant we were at the edge of the cliff, and a foot or so below us was spread the dense, impenetrable blanket of mist. I stopped and hesitated, for the next step might be my last.

"We can't be worse off, so God help us," said Emma, and without waiting for me to lead her she swung herself over the edge.

To my intense relief I heard her alight within a few feet, and followed immediately. Now I was at her side, and now we were scrambling and slipping down the precipitous and rocky slope as swiftly as the dense wet fog would let us. I believe that our escape was quite unnoticed. The guard was watching the murder of the merchant, or, if he saw us, he did not venture to leave the carriage door, and the priest who had accepted some offer which was made to him, probably that his life would be spared if he consented to give absolution to the murderers, was kneeling on the ground, his face hidden in his hands.

As we went the mist grew thinner, and we could see that we were travelling down a steep spur of the precipice, which to our left was quite sheer, and that at the foot of it was a wide plain thickly but not densely covered with trees. In ten minutes we were at the bottom, and as we could neither see nor hear any sign of pursuers we paused for an instant to rest.

Not five yards from us the cliff was broken away, and so straight that a cat could not have climbed it.

"We chose our place well," I said pointing upwards.

"No," Emma answered, "we did not choose; it was chosen for us."

As she spoke a muffled and terrifying sound of agony reached us from above, and then, in the layers of vapour that still stretched between us and the sky, we perceived something huge rushing swiftly down. It appeared; it drew near; it struck, and fell to pieces like a shattered glass. We ran to look, and there before us were the fragments of the diligence, and among them the mangled corpses of five of our fellow-travellers.

This was the fate that we had escaped.

"Oh! for God's sake come away," moaned Emma, and sick with horror we turned and ran, or rather reeled, into the shelter of the trees upon the plain.

CHAPTER II

THE HACIENDA

"What are those?" said Emma presently, pointing to some animals that were half hidden by a clump of wild bananas. I looked and saw that they were two of the mules which the brigands had cut loose from the diligence. There could be no mistake about this, for the harness still hung to them.

"Can you ride?" I asked.

She nodded her head. Then we set to work. Having caught the mules without difficulty, I took off their superfluous harness and put her on the back of one of them, mounting the other myself. There was no time to lose, and we both of us knew it. Just as we were starting I heard a voice behind me calling "senor." Drawing the pistol from my pocket, I swung round to find myself confronted by a Mexican.

"No shoot, senor," he said in broken English, for this man had served upon an American ship, "Me driver, Antonio. My mate go down there," and he pointed to the precipice; "he dead, me not hurt. You run from bad men, me run too, for presently they come look. Where you go?"

"To Mexico," I answered.

"No get Mexico, senor; bad men watch road and kill you with machete so," and he made a sweep with his knife, adding "they not want you live tell soldiers."

"Listen," said Emma. "Do you know the hacienda, Concepcion, by the town of San Jose?"

"Yes, senora, know it well, the hacienda of Senor Gomez; bring you there to-morrow."

"Then show the way," I said, and we started towards the hills.

All that day we travelled over mountains as fast as the mules could carry us, Antonio trotting by our side. At sundown, having seen nothing more of the brigands, who, I suppose, took it for granted that we were dead or were too idle to follow us far, we reached an Indian hut, where we contrived to buy some wretched food consisting of black frijole beans and tortilla cakes. That night we slept in a kind of hovel made of open poles with a roof of faggots through which the water dropped on us, for it rained persistently for several hours. To be more accurate, Emma slept, for my nerves were too shattered by the recollection of our adventure with the brigands to allow me to close my eyes.

I could not rid my mind of the vision of that coach, broken like an eggshell, and of those shattered shapes within it that this very morning had been men full of life and plans, but who to-night were— what? Nor was it easy to forget that but for the merest chance I might have been one of their company wherever it was gathered now. To a man with a constitutional objection to every form of violence, and, at any rate in those days, no desire to search out the secrets of Death before his time, the thought was horrible.

Leaving the shelter at dawn I found Antonio and the Indian who owned the hut conversing together in the reeking mist with their serapes thrown across their mouths, which few Mexicans leave uncovered until after the sun is up. Inflammation of the lungs is the disease they dread more than any other, and the thin night air engenders it.

"What is it, Antonio?" I asked. "Are the brigands after us?"

"No, senor, hope brigands not come now. This senor say much sick San Jose."

I answered that I was very sorry to hear it, but that I meant to go on; indeed, I think that it was only terror of the brigands coupled with the promise of a considerable reward which persuaded him to do so, though, owing to my ignorance of Spanish and his very slight knowledge of English, precisely what he feared I could not discover. In the end we started, and towards evening Antonio pointed out to us the hacienda of Concepcion, a large white building standing on a hill which overshadowed San Jose, a straggling little place, half-town, half-village, with a population of about 3,000 inhabitants.

Just as, riding along the rough cobble-paved road, we reached the entrance to the town, I heard shouts, and, turning, saw two mounted men with rifles in their hands apparently calling to us to come back. Taking it for granted that these were the brigands following us up, although, as I afterwards discovered, they were in fact rurales or cavalry-police, despite the remonstrances of Antonio I urged the jaded mules forward at a gallop. Thereupon the rurales, who had pulled up at a spot marked by a white stone, turned and rode away.

We were now passing down the central street of the town, which I noticed seemed very deserted. As we drew near to the plaza or market square we met a cart drawn by two mules and led by a man who had a serape wrapped about his nose and mouth as though it were still the hour before the dawn. Over the contents of this cart a black cloth was thrown, beneath which were outlined shapes that suggested— but, no, it could not be. Only why did Antonio cross himself and mutter Muerte! or some such word?

Now we were in the plaza. This plaza, where in happier times the band would play, for all Mexicans are musical, and the population of San Jose was wont to traffic in the day and enjoy itself at night, was bordered by an arched colonnade. In its centre stood a basin of water flowing from a stone fountain of quaint and charming design.

"Look at all those people sleeping," said Emma, as we passed five or six forms that, very small and quiet, lay each under a blanket beneath one of the arches. "Why, there are a lot more just lying down over there. What funny folk to go to bed in public in the afternoon," and she pointed to a number of men, women and children who seemed to be getting up, throwing themselves down and turning round and round upon mattresses and beds of leaves in the shadow of the arcade which we approached.

Presently we were within three paces of this arcade, and as we rode up an aged hag drew a blanket from one of the prostrate forms, revealing a young woman, over whom she proceeded to pour water that she had drawn from a fountain. One glance was enough for me. The poor creature's face was shapeless with confluent smallpox, and her body a sight which I will not describe. I, who was a doctor, could not be mistaken, although, as it chanced, I had never seen a case of smallpox before. The truth is that, although I have no fear of any other human ailment, smallpox has always terrified me.

For this I am not to blame. The fear is a part of my nature, instilled into it doubtless by the shock which my mother received before my birth when she learned that her husband had been attacked by this horrible sickness. So great and vivid was my dread that I refused a very good appointment at a smallpox hospital, and, although I had several opportunities of attending these cases, I declined to undertake them, and on this account suffered somewhat in reputation among those who knew the facts. Indeed, my natural abhorrence went even further, as, to this day, it is only with something of an effort that I can bring myself to inspect the vesicles caused by vaccination. Whether this is because of their similarity to those of smallpox, or owing to the natural association which exists between them, I cannot tell. That it is real enough, however, may be judged by the fact that, terrified as I was at smallpox, and convinced as I have always been of the prophylactic power of vaccination, I could never force myself—until an occasion to be told of—to submit to it. In infancy, no doubt, I was vaccinated, for the operation has left a small and very faint cicatrix on my arm, but infantile vaccination, if unrepeated, is but a feeble protection in later life.

Unconsciously I pulled upon the bridle, and the tired mule stopped. "Malignant smallpox!" I muttered, "and that fool is trying to treat it with cold water!"[*]

[*] Readers of Prescott may remember that when this terrible disease was first introduced by a negro slave of Navaez, and killed out millions of the population of Mexico, the unfortunate Aztecs tried to treat it with cold water. Oddly enough, when, some years ago, the writer was travelling in a part of Mexico where smallpox was prevalent, it came to his notice that this system is still followed among the Indians, as they allege, with good results.

The old woman looked up and saw me. "Si, Senor Inglese," she said with a ghastly smile, "viruela, viruela!" and she went on gabbling something which I could not understand.

"She say," broke in Antonio, "nearly quarter people dead and plenty sick."

"For Heaven's sake, let us get out of this," I said to Emma, who, seated on the other mule, was staring horror-struck at the sight.

"Oh!" she said, "you are a doctor; can't you help the poor things?"

"What! and leave you to shift for yourself?"

"Never mind me, Dr. Therne. I can go on to the hacienda, or if you like I will stay too; I am not afraid, I was revaccinated last year."

"Don't be foolish," I answered roughly. "I could not dream of exposing you to such risks, also it is impossible for me to do any good here alone and without medicines. Come on at once," and seizing her mule by the bridle I led it along the road that ran through the town towards the hacienda on the height above.

Ten minutes later we were riding in the great courtyard. The place seemed strangely lifeless and silent; indeed, the plaintive mewing of a cat was the only sound to be heard. Presently, however, a dog appeared out of an open doorway. It was a large animal of the mastiff breed, such as might have been expected to bark and become aggressive to strangers. But this it did not do; indeed, it ran forward and greeted us affectionately. We dismounted and knocked at the double door, but no one answered. Finally we entered, and the truth became clear to us—the hacienda was deserted. A little burial ground attached to the chapel told us why, for in it were several freshly-made graves, evidently of peons or other servants, and in an enclosure, where lay interred some departed members of the Gomez family, another unsodded mound. We discovered afterwards that it was that of the Senor Gomez, Emma's uncle by marriage.

"The footsteps of smallpox," I said, pointing to the graves; "we must go on."

Emma was too overcome to object, for she believed that it was her aunt who slept beneath that mound, so once more we mounted the weary mules. But we did not get far. Within half a mile of the hacienda we were met by two armed rurales, who told us plainly that if we attempted to go further they would shoot.

Then we understood. We had penetrated a smallpox cordon, and must stop in it until forty days after the last traces of the disease had vanished. This, in a wild part of Mexico, where at that time vaccination was but little practised and medical assistance almost entirely lacking, would not be until half or more of the unprotected population was dead and many of the remainder were blinded, deafened or disfigured.

Back we crept to the deserted hacienda, and there in this hideous nest of smallpox we took up our quarters, choosing out of the many in the great pile sleeping rooms that had evidently not been used for months or years. Food we did not lack, for sheep and goats were straying about untended, while in the garden we found fruit and vegetables in plenty, and in the pantries flour and other stores.

At first Emma was dazed and crushed by fatigue and emotion, but she recovered her spirits after a night's sleep and on learning from Antonio, who was told it by some peon, that it was not her aunt that the smallpox had killed, but her uncle by marriage, whom she had never seen. Having no fear of the disease, indeed, she became quite resigned and calm, for the strangeness and novelty of the position absorbed and interested her. Also, to my alarm, it excited her philanthropic instincts, her great idea being to turn the hacienda into a convalescent smallpox hospital, of which she was to be the nurse and I the doctor. Indeed she refused to abandon this mad scheme until I pointed out that in the event of any of our patients dying, most probably we should both be murdered for wizards with the evil eye. As a matter of fact, without medicine or assistance we could have done little or nothing.

Oh, what a pestilence was that of which for three weeks or so we were the daily witnesses, for from the flat roof of the hacienda we could see straight on to the plaza of the little town. And when at night we could not see, still we could hear the wails of the dying and bereaved, the eternal clang of the church bells, rung to scare away the demon of disease, and the midnight masses chanted by the priests, that grew faint and fainter as their brotherhood dwindled, until at last they ceased. And so it went on in the tainted, stricken place until the living were not enough to bury the dead, or to do more than carry food and water to the sick.

It would seem that about twelve years before a philanthropic American enthusiast, armed with a letter of recommendation from whoever at that date was President of Mexico, and escorted by a small guard, descended upon San Jose to vaccinate it. For a few days all went well, for the enthusiast was a good doctor, who understood how to treat ophthalmia and to operate for squint, both of which complaints were prevalent in San Jose. Then his first vaccination patients developed vesicles, and the trouble began. The end of the matter was that the local priests, a very ignorant class of men, interfered, declaring that smallpox was a trial sent from Heaven which it was impious to combat, and that in any case vaccination was the worse disease of the two.

As the viruela had scarcely visited San Jose within the memory of man and the vesicles looked alarming, the population, true children of the Church, agreed with their pastors, and, from purely religious motives, hooted and stoned the philanthropic "Americano" and his guard out of the district. Now they and their innocent children were reaping the fruits of the piety of these conscientious objectors.

After the first fortnight this existence in an atmosphere of disease became absolutely terrible to me. Not an hour of the day passed that I did not imagine some symptom of smallpox, and every morning when we met at breakfast I glanced at Emma with anxiety. The shadow of the thing lay deep upon my nerves, and I knew well that if I stopped there much longer I should fall a victim to it in the body. In this emergency, by means of Antonio, I opened negotiations with the officer of the rurales, and finally, after much secret bargaining, it was arranged that in consideration of a sum of two hundred dollars—for by good luck I had escaped from the brigands with my money—our flight through the cordon of guards should not be observed in the darkness.

We were to start at nine o'clock on a certain night. At a quarter to that hour I went to the stable to see that everything was ready, and in the courtyard outside of it found Antonio seated against the water tank groaning and writhing with pains in the back. One looked showed me that he had developed the usual symptoms, so, feeling that no time was to be lost, I saddled the mules myself and took them round.

"Where is Antonio?" asked Emma as she mounted.

"He has gone on ahead," I answered, "to be sure that the road is clear; he will meet us beyond the mountains."

Poor Antonio! I wonder what became of him; he was a good fellow, and I hope that he recovered. It grieved me much to leave him, but after all I had my own safety to think of, and still more that of Emma, who had grown very dear to me. Perhaps one day I shall find him "beyond the mountains," but, if so, that is a meeting from which I expect no joy.

The rest of our journey was strange enough, but it has nothing to do with this history. Indeed, I have only touched upon these long past adventures in a far land because they illustrate the curious fatality by the workings of which every important event of my life has taken place under the dreadful shadow of smallpox. I was born under that shadow, I wedded under it, I—but the rest shall be told in its proper order.

In the end we reached Mexico City in safety, and there Emma and I were married. Ten days later we were on board ship steaming for England.

CHAPTER III

SIR JOHN BELL

Now it is that I came to the great and terrible event of my life, which in its result turned me into a false witness and a fraud, and bound upon my spirit a weight of blood-guiltiness greater than a man is often called upon to bear. As I have not scrupled to show I have constitutional weaknesses—more, I am a sinner, I know it; I have sinned against the code of my profession, and have preached a doctrine I knew to be false, using all my skill and knowledge to confuse and pervert the minds of the ignorant. And yet I am not altogether responsible for these sins, which in truth in the first place were forced upon me by shame and want and afterwards by the necessities of my ambition. Indeed, in that dark and desperate road of deceit there is no room to turn; the step once taken can never be retraced.

But if I have sinned, how much greater is the crime of the man who swore away my honour and forced me through those gateways? Surely on his head and not on mine should rest the burden of my deeds; yet he prospered all his life, and I have been told that his death was happy and painless. This man's career furnishes one of the few arguments that to my sceptical mind suggest the existence of a place of future reward and punishment, for how is it possible that so great a villain should reap no fruit from his rich sowing of villainy? If it is possible, then verily this world is the real hell wherein the wicked are lords and the good their helpless and hopeless slaves.

Emma Becker when she became my wife brought with her a small dowry of about five thousand dollars, or a thousand pounds, and this sum we both agreed would be best spent in starting me in professional life. It was scarcely sufficient to enable me to buy a practice of the class which I desired, so I determined that I would set to work to build one up, as with my ability and record I was certain that I could do. By preference, I should have wished to begin in London, but there the avenue to success is choked, and I had not the means to wait until by skill and hard work I could force my way along it.

London being out of the question, I made up my mind to try my fortune in the ancient city of Dunchester, where the name of Therne was still remembered, as my grandfather and father had practised there before me. I journeyed to the place and made inquiries, to find that, although there were plenty of medical men of a sort, there was only one whose competition I had cause to fear. Of the others, some had no presence, some no skill, and some no character; indeed, one of them was known to drink.

With Sir John Bell, whose good fortune it was to be knighted in recognition of his attendance upon a royal duchess who chanced to contract the measles while staying in the town, the case was different. He began life as assistant to my father, and when his health failed purchased the practice from him for a miserable sum, which, as he was practically in possession, my father was obliged to accept. From that time forward his success met with no check. By no means a master of his art, Sir John supplied with assurance what he lacked in knowledge, and atoned for his mistakes by the readiness of a bluff and old-fashioned sympathy that was transparent to few.

In short, if ever a faux bonhomme existed, Sir John Bell was the man. Needless to say he was as popular as he was prosperous. Such of the practice of Dunchester as was worth having soon fell into his hands, and few indeed were the guineas that slipped out of his fingers into the pocket of a poorer brother. Also, he had a large consulting connection in the county. But if his earnings were great so were his spendings, for it was part of his system to accept civic and magisterial offices and to entertain largely in his official capacities. This meant that the money went out as fast as it came in, and that, however much was earned, more was always needed.

When I visited Dunchester to make inquiries I made a point of calling on Sir John, who received me in his best "heavy-father" manner, taking care to inform me that he was keeping Lord So-and-so waiting in his consulting-room in order to give me audience. Going straight to the point, I told him that I thought of starting to practise in Dunchester, which information, I could see, pleased him little.

"Of course, my dear boy," he said, "you being your father's son I should be delighted, and would do everything in my power to help you, but at the same time I must point out that were Galen, or Jenner, or Harvey to reappear on earth, I doubt if they could make a decent living in Dunchester."

"All the same, I mean to have a try, Sir John," I answered cheerfully. "I suppose you do not want an assistant, do you?"

"Let me see; I think you said you were married, did you not?"

"Yes," I answered, well knowing that Sir John, having disposed of his elder daughter to an incompetent person of our profession, who had become the plague of his life, was desirous of putting the second to better use.

"No, my dear boy, no, I have an assistant already," and he sighed, this time with genuine emotion. "If you come here you will have to stand upon your own legs."

"Quite so, Sir John, but I shall still hope for a few crumbs from the master's table."

"Yes, yes, Therne, in anything of that sort you may rely upon me," and he bowed me out with an effusive smile.

"— to poison the crumbs," I thought to myself, for I was never for one moment deceived as to this man's character.

A fortnight later Emma and I came to Dunchester and took up our abode in a quaint red-brick house of the Queen Anne period, which we hired for a not extravagant rent of 80 pounds a year. Although the position of this house was not fashionable, nothing could have been more suitable from a doctor's point of view, as it stood in a little street near the market-place and absolutely in the centre of the city. Moreover, it had two beautiful reception chambers on the ground floor, oak-panelled, and with carved Adam's mantelpieces, which made excellent waiting-rooms for patients. Some time passed, however, and our thousand pounds, in which the expense of furnishing had made a considerable hole, was melting rapidly before those rooms were put to a practical use. Both I and my wife did all that we could to get practice. We called upon people who had been friends of my father and grandfather; we attended missionary and other meetings of a non-political character; regardless of expense we went so far as to ask old ladies to tea.

They came, they drank the tea and inspected the new furniture; one of them even desired to see my instruments and when, fearing to give offence, I complied and produced them, she remarked that they were not nearly so nice as dear Sir John's, which had ivory handles. Cheerfully would I have shown her that if the handles were inferior the steel was quite serviceable, but I swallowed my wrath and solemnly explained that it was not medical etiquette for a young doctor to use ivory.

Beginning to despair, I applied for one or two minor appointments in answer to advertisements inserted by the Board of Guardians and other public bodies. In each case was I not only unsuccessful, but men equally unknown, though with a greatly inferior college and hospital record, were chosen over my head. At length, suspecting that I was not being fairly dealt by, I made inquiries to discover that at the bottom of all this ill success was none other than Sir John Bell. It appeared that in several instances, by the shrugs of his thick shoulders and shakes of his ponderous head, he had prevented my being employed. Indeed, in the case of the public bodies, with all of which he had authority either as an official or as an honorary adviser, he had directly vetoed my appointment by the oracular announcement that, after ample inquiry among medical friends in London, he had satisfied himself that I was not a suitable person for the post.

When I had heard this and convinced myself that it was substantially true—for I was always too cautious to accept the loose and unsifted gossip of a provincial town—I think that for the first time in my life I experienced the passion of hate towards a human being. Why should this man who was so rich and powerful thus devote his energies to the destruction of a brother practitioner who was struggling and poor? At the time I set it down to pure malice, into which without doubt it blossomed at last, not understanding that in the first place on Sir John's part it was in truth terror born of his own conscious mediocrity. Like most inferior men, he was quick to recognise his master, and, either in the course of our conversations or through inquiries that he made concerning me, he had come to the conclusion that so far as professional ability was concerned I was his master. Therefore, being a creature of petty and dishonest mind, he determined to crush me before I could assert myself.

Now, having ascertained all this beyond reasonable doubt, there were three courses open to me: to make a public attack upon Sir John, to go away and try my fortune elsewhere, or to sit still and await events. A more impetuous man would have adopted the first of these alternatives, but my experience of life, confirmed as it was by the advice of Emma, who was a shrewd and far-seeing woman, soon convinced me that if I did so I should have no more chance of success than would an egg which undertook a crusade against a brick wall. Doubtless the egg might stain the wall and gather the flies of gossip about its stain, but the end of it must be that the wall would still stand, whereas the egg would no longer be an egg. The second plan had more attractions, but my resources were now too low to allow me to put it into practice. Therefore, having no other choice, I was forced to adopt the third, and, exercising that divine patience which characterises the Eastern nations but is so lacking in our own, to attend humbly upon fate until it should please it to deal to me a card that I could play.

In time fate dealt to me that card and my long suffering was rewarded, for it proved a very ace of trumps. It happened thus.

About a year after I arrived in Dunchester I was elected a member of the City Club. It is a pleasant place, where ladies are admitted to lunch, and I used it a good deal in the hope of making acquaintances who might be useful to me. Among the habitues of this club was a certain Major Selby, who, having retired from the army and being without occupation, was generally to be found in the smoking or billiard room with a large cigar between his teeth and a whisky and soda at his side. In face, the Major was florid and what people call healthy-looking, an appearance that to a doctor's eye very often conveys no assurance of physical well-being. Being a genial-mannered man, he would fall into conversation with whoever might be near to him, and thus I came to be slightly acquainted with him. In the course of our chats he frequently mentioned his ailments, which, as might be expected in the case of such a luxurious liver, were gouty in their origin.

One afternoon when I was sitting alone in the smoking-room, Major Selby came in and limped to an armchair.

"Hullo, Major, have you got the gout again?" I asked jocosely.

"No, doctor; at least that pompous old beggar, Bell, says I haven't. My leg has been so confoundedly painful and stiff for the last few days that I went to see him this morning, but he told me that it was only a touch of rheumatism, and gave me some stuff to rub it with."

"Oh, and did he look at your leg?"

"Not he. He says that he can tell what my ailments are with the width of the street between us."

"Indeed," I said, and some other men coming in the matter dropped.

Four days later I was in the club at the same hour, and again Major Selby entered. This time he walked with considerable difficulty, and I noticed an expression of pain and malaise upon his rubicund countenance. He ordered a whisky and soda from the servant, and then sat down near me.

"Rheumatism no better, Major?" I asked.

"No, I went to see old Bell about it again yesterday, but he pooh-poohs it and tells me to go on rubbing in the liniment and get the footman to help when I am tired. Well, I obeyed orders, but it hasn't done me much good, and how the deuce rheumatism can give a fellow a bruise on the leg, I don't know."

"A bruise on the leg?" I said astonished.

"Yes, a bruise on the leg, and, if you don't believe me, look here," and, dragging up his trouser, he showed me below the knee a large inflamed patch of a dusky hue, in the centre of which one of the veins could be felt to be hard and swollen.

"Has Sir John Bell seen that?" I asked.

"Not he. I wanted him to look at it, but he was in a hurry, and said I was just like an old woman with a sore on show, so I gave it up."

"Well, if I were you, I'd go home and insist upon his coming to look at it."

"What do you mean, doctor?" he asked growing alarmed at my manner.

"Oh, it is a nasty place, that is all; and I think that when Sir John has seen it, he will tell you to keep quiet for a few days."

Major Selby muttered something uncomplimentary about Sir John, and then asked me if I would come home with him.

"I can't do that as a matter of medical etiquette, but I'll see you into a cab. No, I don't think I should drink that whisky if I were you, you want to keep yourself cool and quiet."

So Major Selby departed in his cab and I went home, and, having nothing better to do, turned up my notes on various cases of venous thrombosis, or blood-clot in the veins, which I had treated at one time or another.

While I was still reading them there came a violent ring at the bell, followed by the appearance of a very agitated footman, who gasped out:—

"Please, sir, come to my master, Major Selby, he has been taken ill."

"I can't, my good man," I answered, "Sir John Bell is his doctor."

"I have been to Sir John's, sir, but he has gone away for two days to attend a patient in the country, and the Major told me to come for you."

Then I hesitated no longer. As we hurried to the house, which was close at hand, the footman told me that the Major on reaching home took a cup of tea and sent for a cab to take him to Sir John Bell. As he was in the act of getting into the cab, suddenly he fell backwards and was picked up panting for breath, and carried into the dining-room. By this time we had reached the house, of which the door was opened as we approached it by Mrs. Selby herself, who seemed in great distress.

"Don't talk now, but take me to your husband," I said, and was led into the dining-room, where the unfortunate man lay groaning on the sofa.

"Glad you've come," he gasped. "I believe that fool, Bell, has done for me."

Asking those present in the room, a brother and a grown-up son of the patient, to stand back, I made a rapid examination; then I wrote a prescription and sent it round to the chemist—it contained ammonia, I remember—and ordered hot fomentations to be placed upon the leg. While these matters were being attended to I went with the relations into another room.

"What is the matter with him, doctor?" asked Mrs. Selby.

"It is, I think, a case of what is called blood-clot, which has formed in the veins of the leg," I answered. "Part of this clot has been detached by exertion, or possibly by rubbing, and, travelling upwards, has become impacted in one of the pulmonary arteries."

"Is it serious?" asked the poor wife.

"Of course we must hope for the best," I said; "but it is my duty to tell you that I do not myself think Major Selby will recover; how long he will last depends upon the size of the clot which has got into the artery."

"Oh, this is ridiculous," broke in Mr. Selby. "My brother has been under the care of Sir John Bell, the ablest doctor in Dunchester, who told him several times that he was suffering from nothing but rheumatism, and now this gentleman starts a totally different theory, which, if it were true, would prove Sir John to be a most careless and incompetent person."

"I am very sorry," I answered; "I can only hope that Sir John is right and I am wrong. So that there may be no subsequent doubt as to what I have said, with your leave I will write down my diagnosis and give it to you."

When this was done I returned to the patient, and Mr. Selby, taking my diagnosis, telegraphed the substance of it to Sir John Bell for his opinion. In due course the answer arrived from Sir John, regretting that there was no train by which he could reach Dunchester that night, giving the name of another doctor who was to be called in, and adding, incautiously enough, "Dr. Therne's diagnosis is purely theoretical and such as might be expected from an inexperienced man."

Meanwhile the unfortunate Major was dying. He remained conscious to the last, and, in spite of everything that I could do, suffered great pain. Amongst other things he gave an order that a post-mortem examination should be made to ascertain the cause of his death.

When Mr. Selby had read the telegram from Sir John he handed it to me, saying, "It is only fair that you should see this."

I read it, and, having asked for and obtained a copy, awaited the arrival of the other doctor before taking my departure. When at length he came Major Selby was dead.

Two days later the post-mortem was held. There were present at it Sir John Bell, myself, and the third medico, Dr. Jeffries. It is unnecessary to go into details, but in the issue I was proved to be absolutely right. Had Sir John taken the most ordinary care and precaution his patient need not have died—indeed, his death was caused by the treatment. The rubbing of the leg detached a portion of the clot, that might easily have been dissolved by rest and local applications. As it was, it went to his lung, and he died.

When he saw how things were going, Sir John tried to minimise matters, but, unfortunately for him, I had my written diagnosis and a copy of his telegram, documents from which he could not escape. Nor could he deny the results of the post-mortem, which took place in the presence and with the assistance of the third practitioner, a sound and independent, though not a very successful, man.

When everything was over there was something of a scene. Sir John asserted that my conduct had been impertinent and unprofessional. I replied that I had only done my duty and appealed to Dr. Jeffries, who remarked drily that we had to deal not with opinions and theories but with facts and that the facts seemed to bear me out. On learning the truth, the relatives, who until now had been against me, turned upon Sir John and reproached him in strong terms, after which they went away leaving us face to face. There was an awkward silence, which I broke by saying that I was sorry to have been the unwilling cause of this unpleasantness.

"You may well be sorry, sir," Sir John answered in a cold voice that was yet alive with anger, "seeing that by your action you have exposed me to insult, I who have practised in this city for over thirty years, and who was your father's partner before you were in your cradle. Well, it is natural to youth to be impertinent. To-day the laugh is yours, Dr. Therne, to-morrow it may be mine; so good-afternoon, and let us say no more about it," and brushing by me rudely he passed from the house.

I followed him into the street watching his thick square form, of which even the back seemed to express sullen anger and determination. At a distance of a few yards stood the brother of the dead man, Mr. Selby, talking to Dr. Jeffries, one of whom made some remark that caught Sir John's ear. He stopped as though to answer, then, changing his mind, turned his head and looked back at me. My sight is good and I could see his face clearly; on it was a look of malignity that was not pleasant to behold.

"I have made a bad enemy," I thought to myself; "well, I am in the right; one must take risks in life, and it is better to be hated than despised."

Major Selby was a well-known and popular man, whose sudden death had excited much sympathy and local interest, which were intensified when the circumstances connected with it became public property.

On the following day the leading city paper published a report of the results of the post-mortem, which doubtless had been furnished by the relatives, and with it an editorial note.

In this paragraph I was spoken of in very complimentary terms; my medical distinctions were alluded to, and the confident belief was expressed that Dunchester would not be slow to avail itself of my skill and talent. Sir John Bell was not so lightly handled. His gross error of treatment in the case of the deceased was, it is true, slurred over, but some sarcastic and disparaging remarks were aimed at him under cover of comparison between the old and the new school of medical practitioners.

CHAPTER IV

STEPHEN STRONG GOES BAIL

Great are the uses of advertisement! When I went into my consulting-room after breakfast that day I found three patients waiting to see me, one of them a member of a leading family in the city.

Here was the beginning of my success. Whatever time may remain to me, to-day in a sense my life is finished. I am a broken-hearted and discomfited man, with little more to fear and nothing to hope. Therefore I may be believed when I say that in these pages I set down the truth and nothing but the truth, not attempting to palliate my conduct where it has been wrong, nor to praise myself even when praise may have been due. Perhaps, then, it will not be counted conceit when I write that in my best days I was really a master of my trade. To my faculty for diagnosis I have, I think, alluded; it amounted to a gift—a touch or two of my fingers would often tell me what other doctors could not discover by prolonged examination. To this I added a considerable mastery of the details of my profession, and a sympathetic insight into character, which enabled me to apply my knowledge to the best advantage.

When a patient came to me and told me that his symptoms were this or that or the other, I began by studying the man and forming my own conclusions as to his temperament, character, and probable past. It was this method of mine of studying the individual as a whole and his ailment as something springing from and natural to his physical and spiritual entity that, so far as general principles can be applied to particular instances, often gave me a grip of the evil, and enabled me, by dealing with the generating cause, to strike at its immediate manifestation. My axiom was that in the human subject mind is king; the mind commands, the body obeys. From this follows the corollary that the really great doctor, however trivial the complaint, should always begin by trying to understand the mind of his patient, to follow the course of its workings, and estimate their results upon his physical nature.

Necessarily there are many cases to which this rule does not seem to apply, those of contagious sickness, for instance, or those of surgery, resulting from accident. And yet even there it does apply, for the condition of the mind may predispose to infection, and to recovery or collapse in the instance of the sufferer from injuries. But these questions of predisposition and consequence are too great to argue here, though even the most rule-of-thumb village practitioner, with a black draught in one hand and a pot of ointment in the other, will agree that they admit of a wide application.

At least it is to these primary principles over and above my technical skill that I attribute my success while I was successful. That at any rate was undoubted. Day by day my practice grew, to such an extent indeed, that on making up my books at the end of the second year, I found that during the preceding twelve months I had taken over 900 pounds in fees and was owed about 300 pounds more. Most of this balance, however, I wrote off as a bad debt, since I made it a custom never to refuse a patient merely because he might not be able to pay me. I charged large fees, for a doctor gains nothing by being cheap, but if I thought it inexpedient I did not attempt to collect them.

After this matter of the inquest on Major Selby the relations between Sir John Bell and myself were very strained—in fact, for a while he refused to meet me in consultation. When this happened, without attempting to criticise his action, I always insisted upon retiring from the case, saying that it was not for me, a young man, to stand in the path of one of so great experience and reputation. As might be expected this moderation resulted in my triumph, for the time came when Sir John thought it wise to waive his objections and to recognise me professionally. Then I knew that I had won the day, for in that equal field I was his master. Never once that I can remember did he venture to reverse or even to cavil at my treatment, at any rate in my presence, though doubtless he criticised it freely elsewhere.

And so I flourished, and as I waxed he waned, until, calculating my chances with my wife, I was able to prophesy that if no accident or ill-chance occurred to stop me, within another three years I should be the leading practitioner in Dunchester, while Sir John Bell would occupy the second place.

But I had reckoned without his malice, for, although I knew this to be inveterate, I had underrated its probable effects, and in due course the ill-chance happened. It came about in this wise.

When we had been married something over two years my wife found herself expecting to become a mother. As the event drew near she expressed great anxiety that I should attend upon her. To this, however, I objected strenuously—first, because I cannot bear to see any one to whom I am attached suffer pain, and, secondly, because I knew that my affection and personal anxiety would certainly unnerve me. Except in cases of the utmost necessity no man, in my opinion, should doctor himself or his family. Whilst I was wondering how to arrange matters I chanced to meet Sir John Bell in consultation. After our business was over, developing an unusual geniality of manner, he proposed to walk a little way with me.

"I understand, my dear Therne," he said, "that there is an interesting event expected in your family."

I replied that this was so.

"Well," he went on, "though we may differ on some points, I am sure there is one upon which we shall agree—that no man should doctor his own flesh and blood. Now, look here, I want you to let me attend upon your good wife. However much you go-ahead young fellows may turn up your noses at us old fossils, I think you will admit that by this time I ought to be able to show a baby into the world, especially as I had the honour of performing that office for yourself, my young friend."

For a moment I hesitated. What Sir John said was quite true; he was a sound and skilful obstetrician of the old school. Moreover, he evidently intended to hold out the olive branch by this kind offer, which I felt that I ought to accept. Already, having conquered in the fray, I forgave him the injuries that he had worked me. It is not in my nature to bear unnecessary malice—indeed, I hate making or having an enemy. And yet I hesitated, not from any premonition or presentiment of the dreadful events that were to follow, but simply because of my wife's objection to being attended by any one but myself. I thought of advancing this in excuse of a refusal, but checked myself, because I was sure that he would interpret it as a rebuff, and in consequence hate me more bitterly than ever. So in the end I accepted his offer gratefully, and we parted.

When I told Emma she was a little upset, but being a sensible woman she soon saw the force of my arguments and fell in with the situation. In truth, unselfish creature that she was, she thought more of the advantage that would accrue to me by this formal burying of the hatchet than of her own prejudices or convenience.

The time came and with it Sir John Bell, large, sharp-eyed, and jocose. In due course and under favourable conditions a daughter was born to me, a very beautiful child, fair like her mother, but with my dark eyes.

I think it was on the fourth day from the birth of the child that I went after luncheon to see my wife, who so far had done exceedingly well. I found her depressed, and she complained of headache. Just then the servant arrived saying that I was wanted in the consulting-room, so I kissed Emma and, after arranging her bed-clothing and turning her over so that she might lie more comfortably, I hurried downstairs, telling her that she had better go to sleep.

While I was engaged with my visitor Sir John Bell came to see my wife. Just as the patient had gone and Sir John was descending the stairs a messenger hurried in with a note summoning me instantly to attend upon Lady Colford, the wife of a rich banker and baronet who, I knew, was expecting her first confinement. Seizing my bag I started, and, as I reached the front door, I thought that I heard Sir John, who was now nearly at the foot of the stairs, call out something to me. I answered that I couldn't stop but would see him later, to which I understood him to reply "All right."

This was about three o'clock in the afternoon, but so protracted and anxious was the case of Lady Colford that I did not reach home again till eight. Having swallowed a little food, for I was thoroughly exhausted, I went upstairs to see my wife. Entering the room softly I found that she was asleep, and that the nurse also was dozing on the sofa in the dressing-room. Fearing to disturb them, I kissed her lips, and going downstairs returned at once to Sir Thomas Colford's house, where I spent the entire night in attendance on his wife.

When I came home again about eight o'clock on the following morning it was to find Sir John Bell awaiting me in the consulting-room. A glance at his face told me that there was something dreadfully wrong.

"What is it?" I asked.

"What is it? Why, what I called after you yesterday, only you wouldn't stop to listen, and I haven't known where to find you since. It's puerperal fever, and Heaven knows what gave it to her, for I don't. I thought so yesterday, and this morning I am sure of it."

"Puerperal fever," I muttered, "then I am ruined, whatever happens to Emma."

"Don't talk like that, man," answered Sir John, "she has a capital constitution, and, I daresay, we shall pull her through."

"You don't understand. I have been attending Lady Colford, going straight from Emma's room to her."

Sir John whistled. "Oh, indeed. Certainly, that's awkward. Well, we must hope for the best, and, look you here, when a fellow calls out to you another time just you stop to listen."

To dwell on all that followed would serve no good purpose, and indeed what is the use of setting down the details of so much forgotten misery? In a week my beloved wife was dead, and in ten days Lady Colford had followed her into the darkness. Then it was, that to complete my own destruction, I committed an act of folly, for, meeting Sir John Bell, in my mad grief I was fool enough to tell him I knew that my wife's death, and indirectly that of Lady Colford, were due to his improper treatment and neglect of precautions.

I need not enter into the particulars, but this in fact was the case.

He did not say much in answer to my accusation, but merely replied:—

"I make allowances for you; but, Dr. Therne, it is time that somebody taught you that people's reputations cannot be slandered with impunity. Instead of attacking me I should recommend you to think of defending yourself."

Very soon I learned the meaning of this hint. I think it was within a week of my wife's funeral that I heard that Sir Thomas Colford, together with all his relations and those of the deceased lady, were absolutely furious with me. Awaking from my stupor of grief, I wrote a letter to Sir Thomas expressing my deep regret at the misfortune that I had been the innocent means of bringing upon him. To this letter I received a reply by hand, scrawled upon half a sheet of notepaper. It ran:—

"Sir Thomas Colford is surprised that Dr. Therne should think it worth while to add falsehood to murder."

Then, for the first time, I understood in what light my terrible misfortune was regarded by the public. A few days later I received further enlightenment, this time from the lips of an inspector of police, who called upon me with a warrant of arrest on the charge of having done manslaughter on the body of Dame Blanche Colford.

That night I spent in Dunchester Jail, and next morning I was brought before the bench of magistrates, who held a special session to try my case. The chairman, whom I knew well, very kindly asked me if I did not wish for legal assistance. I replied, "No, I have nothing to defend," which he seemed to think a hard saying, at any rate he looked surprised. On the other side counsel were employed nominally on behalf of the Crown, although in reality the prosecution, which in such a case was unusual if not unprecedented, had been set on foot and undertaken by the Colford family.

The "information" was read by the clerk, in which I was charged with culpable negligence and wilfully doing certain things that caused the death of Blanche Colford. I stood there in the dock listening, and wondering what possible evidence could be adduced against me in support of such a charge. After the formal witnesses, relations and doctors, who testified to my being called in to attend on Lady Colford, to the course of the illness and the cause of death, etc., Sir John Bell was called. "Now," I thought to myself, "this farce will come to an end, for Bell will explain the facts."

The counsel for the prosecution began by asking Sir John various questions concerning the terrible malady known as puerperal fever, and especially with reference to its contagiousness. Then he passed on to the events of the day when I was called in to attend upon Lady Colford. Sir John described how he had visited my late wife, and, from various symptoms which she had developed somewhat suddenly, to his grief and surprise, had come to the conclusion that she had fallen victim to puerperal fever. This evidence, to begin with, was not true, for although he suspected the ailment on that afternoon he was not sure of it until the following morning.

"What happened then, Sir John?" asked the counsel.

"Leaving my patient I hurried downstairs to see Dr. Therne, and found him just stepping from his consulting-room into the hall."

"Did he speak to you?"

"Yes. He said 'How do you do?' and then added, before I could tell him about his wife, 'I am rather in luck to-day; they are calling me in to take Lady Colford's case.' I said I was glad to hear it, but that I thought he had better let some one else attend her ladyship. He looked astonished, and asked why. I said, 'Because, my dear fellow, I am afraid that your wife has developed puerperal fever, and the nurse tells me that you were in her room not long ago.' He replied that it was impossible, as he had looked at her and thought her all right except for a little headache. I said that I trusted that I might be wrong, but if nearly forty years' experience went for anything I was not wrong. Then he flew into a passion, and said that if anything was the matter with his wife it was my fault, as I must have brought the contagion or neglected to take the usual antiseptic precautions. I told him that he should not make such statements without an atom of proof, but, interrupting me, he declared that, fever or no fever, he would attend upon Lady Colford, as he could not afford to throw away the best chance he had ever had. I said, 'My dear fellow, don't be mad. Why, if anything happened to her under the circumstances, I believe that, after I have warned you, you would be liable to be criminally prosecuted for culpable negligence.' 'Thank you,' he answered, 'nothing will happen to her, I know my own business, and I will take the chance of that'; and then, before I could speak again, lifting up his bag from the chair on which he had placed it, he opened the front door and went out."

I will not attempt, especially after this lapse of years, to describe the feelings with which I listened to this amazing evidence. The black wickedness and the cold-blooded treachery of the man overwhelmed and paralysed me, so that when, after some further testimony, the chairman asked me if I had any questions to put to the witness, I could only stammer:—

"It is a lie, an infamous lie!"

"No, no," said the chairman kindly, "if you wish to make a statement, you will have an opportunity of doing so presently. Have you any questions to ask the witness?"

I shook my head. How could I question him on such falsehoods? Then came the nurse, who, amidst a mass of other information, calmly swore that, standing on the second landing, whither she had accompanied Sir John from his patient's room, she heard a lengthy conversation proceeding between him and me, and caught the words, "I will take the chance of that," spoken in my voice.

Again I had no questions to ask, but I remembered that this nurse was a person who for a long while had been employed by Sir John Bell, and one over whom he very probably had some hold.

Then I was asked if I had any witness, but, now that my wife was dead, what witness could I call?—indeed, I could not have called her had she been alive. Then, having been cautioned in the ordinary form, that whatever I said might be given as evidence against me at my trial, I was asked if I wished to make any statement.

I did make a statement of the facts so far as I knew them, adding that the evidence of Sir John Bell and the nurse was a tissue of falsehoods, and that the former had been my constant enemy ever since I began to practise in Dunchester, and more especially since the issue of a certain case, in the treatment of which I had proved him to be wrong. When my statement had been taken down and I had signed it, the chairman, after a brief consultation with his companions, announced that, as those concerned had thought it well to institute this prosecution, in the face of the uncontradicted evidence of Sir John Bell the bench had no option but to send me to take my trial at the Dunchester Assizes, which were to be held on that day month. In order, however, to avoid the necessity of committing me to jail, they would be prepared to take bail for my appearance in a sum of 500 pounds from myself, and 500 pounds, in two sureties of 250 pounds, or one of the whole amount.

Now I looked about me helplessly, for I had no relations in Dunchester, where I had not lived long enough to form friends sufficiently true to be willing to thus identify themselves publicly with a man in great trouble.

"Thank you for your kindness," I said, "but I think that I must go to prison, for I do not know whom to ask to go bail for me."

As I spoke there was a stir at the back of the crowded court, and an ungentle voice called out, "I'll go bail for you, lad."

"Step forward whoever spoke," said the clerk, and a man advanced to the table.

He was a curious and not very healthy-looking person of about fifty years of age, ill-dressed in seedy black clothes and a flaming red tie, with a fat, pale face, a pugnacious mouth, and a bald head, on the top of which isolated hairs stood up stiffly. I knew him by sight, for once he had argued with me at a lecture I gave on sanitary matters, when I was told that he was a draper by trade, and, although his shop was by no means among the most important, that he was believed to be one of the richest men in Dunchester. Also he was a fierce faddist and a pillar of strength to the advanced wing of the Radical party.

"What is your name?" asked a clerk.

"Look you here, young man," he answered, "don't have the impertinence to try your airs and graces on with me. Seeing that you've owed me 24 pounds 3s. 6d. for the last three years for goods supplied, you know well enough what my name is, or if you don't I will show it to you at the bottom of a county court summons."

"It is my duty to ask you your name," responded the disconcerted clerk when the laughter which this sally provoked had subsided.

"Oh, very well. Stephen Strong is my name, and I may tell you that it is good at the bottom of a cheque for any reasonable amount. Well, I'm here to go bail for that young man. I know nothing of him except that I put him on his back in a ditch in an argument we had one night last winter in the reading-room yonder. I don't know whether he infected the lady or whether he didn't, but I do know, that like most of the poisoning calf-worshipping crowd who call themselves Vaccinators, this Bell is a liar, and that if he did, it wasn't his fault because it was God's will that she should die, and he'd a been wrong to try and interfere with Him. So name your sum and I'll stand the shot."

All of this tirade had been said, or rather shouted, in a strident voice and in utter defiance of the repeated orders of the chairman that he should be silent. Mr. Stephen Strong was not a person very amenable to authority. Now, however, when he had finished his say he not only filled in the bail bond but offered to hand up a cheque for 500 pounds then and there.

When it was over I thanked him, but he only answered:—

"Don't you thank me. I do it because I will not see folk locked up for this sort of nonsense about diseases and the like, as though the Almighty who made us don't know when to send sickness and when to keep it away, when to make us live and when to make us die. Now do you want any money to defend yourself with?"

I answered that I did not, and, having thanked him again, we parted without more words, as I was in no mood to enter into an argument with an enthusiast of this hopeless, but to me, convenient nature.

CHAPTER V

THE TRIAL

Although it took place so long ago, I suppose that a good many people still remember the case of "The Queen versus Therne," which attracted a great deal of attention at the time. The prosecution, as I have said, was set on foot by the relations of the deceased Lady Colford, who, being very rich and powerful people, were able to secure the advocacy of one of the most eminent criminal lawyers of the day, with whom were briefed sundry almost equally eminent juniors. Indeed no trouble or expense was spared that could help to ensure my conviction.

On my behalf also appeared a well-known Q.C., and with him two juniors. The judge who tried the case was old and experienced but had the reputation of being severe, and from its very commencement I could see that the perusal of the depositions taken in the magistrates' court, where it will be remembered I was not defended, had undoubtedly biased his mind against me. As for the jury, they were a respectable-looking quiet set of men, who might be relied upon to do justice according to their lights. Of those who were called from the panel and answered to their names two, by the way, were challenged by the Crown and rejected because, I was told, they were professed anti-vaccinationists.

On the appointed day and hour, speaking in a very crowded court, counsel for the Crown opened the case against me, demonstrating clearly that in the pursuit of my own miserable ends I had sacrificed the life of a young, high-placed and lovely fellow-creature, and brought bereavement and desolation upon her husband and family. Then he proceeded to call evidence, which was practically the same as that which had been given before the magistrates, although the husband and Lady Colford's nurse were examined, and, on my behalf, cross-examined at far greater length.

After the adjournment for lunch Sir John Bell was put into the witness-box, where, with a little additional detail, he repeated almost word for word what he had said before. Listening to him my heart sank, for he made an excellent witness, quiet, self-contained, and, to all appearance, not a little affected by the necessity under which he found himself of exposing the evil doings of a brother practitioner. I noticed with dismay also that his evidence produced a deep effect upon the minds of all present, judge and jury not excepted.

Then came the cross-examination, which certainly was a brilliant performance, for under it were shown that from the beginning Sir John Bell had certainly borne me ill-will; that to his great chagrin I had proved myself his superior in a medical controversy, and that the fever which my wife contracted was in all human probability due to his carelessness and want of precautions while in attendance upon her. When this cross-examination was concluded the court rose for the day, and, being on bail, I escaped from the dock until the following morning.

I returned to my house and went up to the nursery to see the baby, who was a very fine and healthy infant. At first I could scarcely bear to look at this child, remembering always that indirectly it had been the cause of its dear mother's death. But now, when I was so lonely, for even those who called themselves my friends had fallen away from me in the time of trial, I felt drawn towards the helpless little thing.

I kissed it and put it back into its cradle, and was about to leave the room when the nurse, a respectable widow woman with a motherly air, asked me straight out what were my wishes about the child and by what name it was to be baptised, seeing that when I was in jail she might not be able to ascertain them. The good woman's question made me wince, but, recognising that in view of eventualities these matters must be arranged, I took a sheet of paper and wrote down my instructions, which were briefly that the child should be named Emma Jane after its mother and mine, and that the nurse, Mrs. Baker, should take it to her cottage, and be paid a weekly sum for its maintenance.

Having settled these disagreeable details I went downstairs, but not to the dinner that was waiting for me, as after the nurse's questions I did not feel equal to facing the other domestics. Leaving the house I walked about the streets seeking some small eating-place where I could dine without being recognised. As I wandered along wearily I heard a harsh voice behind me calling me by name, and, turning, found that the speaker was Mr. Stephen Strong. Even in the twilight there was no possibility of mistaking his flaming red tie.

"You are worried and tired, doctor," said the harsh voice. "Why ain't you with your friends, instead of tramping the streets after that long day in court?"

"Because I have no friends left," I answered, for I had arrived at that stage of humiliation when a man no longer cares to cloak the truth.

A look of pity passed over Mr. Strong's fat face, and the lines about the pugnacious mouth softened a little.

"Is that so?" he said. "Well, young man, you're learning now what happens to those who put their faith in fashionable folk and not in the Lord. Rats can't scuttle from a sinking ship faster than fashionable folk from a friend in trouble. You come along and have a bit of supper with me and my missis. We're humble trades-folk, but, perhaps as things are, you won't mind that."

I accepted Mr. Strong's invitation with gratitude, indeed his kindness touched me. Leading me to his principal shop, we passed through it and down a passage to a sitting-room heavily furnished with solid horsehair-seated chairs and a sofa. In the exact centre of this sofa, reading by the light of a lamp with a pink shade which was placed on a table behind her, sat a prim grey-haired woman dressed in a black silk dress and apron and a lace cap with lappets. I noticed at once that the right lappet was larger than the left. Evidently it had been made so with the design of hiding a patch of affected skin below the ear, which looked to me as though it had been caused by the malady called lupus. I noticed further that the little woman was reading an anti-vaccination tract with a fearful picture of a diseased arm upon its cover.

"Martha," said Mr. Strong, "Dr. Therne, whom they're trying at the court yonder, has come in for supper. Dr. Therne, that's my wife."

Mrs. Strong rose and offered her hand. She was a thin person, with rather refined features, a weak mouth, and kindly blue eyes.

"I'm sure you are welcome," she said in a small monotonous voice. "Any of Stephen's friends are welcome, and more especially those of them who are suffering persecution for the Right."

"That is not exactly my case, madam," I answered, "for if I had done what they accuse me of I should deserve hanging, but I did not do it."

"I believe you, doctor," she said, "for you have true eyes. Also Stephen says so. But in any case the death of the dear young woman was God's will, and if it was God's will, how can you be responsible?"

While I was wondering what answer I should make to this strange doctrine a servant girl announced that supper was ready, and we went into the next room to partake of a meal, plain indeed, but of most excellent quality. Moreover, I was glad to find, unlike his wife, who touched nothing but water, that Mr. Strong did not include teetotalism among his eccentricities. On the contrary, he produced a bottle of really fine port for my especial benefit.

In the course of our conversation I discovered that the Strongs, who had had no children, devoted themselves to the propagation of various "fads." Mr. Strong indeed was anti-everything, but, which is rather uncommon in such a man, had no extraneous delusions; that is to say, he was not a Christian

Scientist, or a Blavatskyist, or a Great Pyramidist. Mrs. Strong, however, had never got farther than anti-vaccination, to her a holy cause, for she set down the skin disease with which she was constitutionally afflicted to the credit, or discredit, of vaccination practised upon her in her youth. Outside of this great and absorbing subject her mind occupied itself almost entirely with that well-known but most harmless of the crazes, the theory that we Anglo-Saxons are the progeny of the ten lost Tribes of Israel.

Steering clear of anti-vaccination, I showed an intelligent sympathy with her views and deductions concerning the ten Tribes, which so pleased the gentle little woman that, forgetting the uncertainty of my future movements, she begged me to come and see her as often as I liked, and in the meanwhile presented me with a pile of literature connected with the supposed wanderings of the Tribes. Thus began my acquaintance with my friend and benefactress, Martha Strong.

At ten o'clock on the following morning I returned to the dock, and the nurse repeated her evidence in corroboration of Sir John's testimony. A searching cross-examination showed her not to be a very trustworthy person, but on this particular point it was impossible to shake her story, because there was no standing ground from which it could be attacked. Then followed some expert evidence whereby, amongst other things, the Crown proved to the jury the fearfully contagious nature of puerperal fever, which closed the case for the prosecution. After this my counsel, reserving his address, called the only testimony I was in a position to produce, that of several witnesses to character and to medical capacity.

When the last of these gentlemen, none of whom were cross-examined, stood down, my counsel addressed the Court, pointing out that my mouth being closed by the law of the land—for this trial took place before the passing of the Criminal Evidence Act—I was unable to go into the box and give on oath my version of what had really happened in this matter. Nor could I produce any witnesses to disprove the story which had been told against me, because, unhappily, no third person was present at the crucial moments. Now, this story rested entirely on the evidence of Sir John Bell and the nurse, and if it was true I must be mad as well as bad, since a doctor of my ability would well know that under the circumstances he would very probably carry contagion, with the result that a promising professional career might be ruined. Moreover, had he determined to risk it, he would have taken extra precautions in the sick-room to which he was called, and this it was proved I had not done. Now the statement made by me before the magistrates had been put in evidence, and in it I said that the tale was an absolute invention on the part of Sir John Bell, and that when I went to see Lady Colford I had no knowledge whatsoever that my wife was suffering from an infectious ailment. This, he submitted, was the true version of the story, and he confidently asked the jury not to blast the career of an able and rising man, but by their verdict to reinstate him in the position which he had temporarily and unjustly lost.

In reply, the leading counsel for the Crown said that it was neither his wish nor his duty to strain the law against me, or to put a worse interpretation upon the facts than they would bear under the strictest scrutiny. He must point out, however, that if the contention of his learned friend were correct, Sir John Bell was one of the wickedest villains who ever disgraced the earth.

In summing up the judge took much the same line. The case, that was of a character upon which it was unusual though perfectly allowable to found a criminal prosecution, he pointed out, rested solely upon the evidence of Sir John Bell, corroborated as it was by the nurse. If that evidence was correct, then, to satisfy my own ambition or greed, I had deliberately risked and, as the issue showed, had taken the life of a lady who in all confidence was entrusted to my care. Incredible as such wickedness might seem, the jury must remember that it was by no means unprecedented. At the same time there was a point that had been scarcely dwelt upon by counsel to which he would call their attention. According to Sir John

Bell's account, it was from his lips that I first learned that my wife was suffering from a peculiarly dangerous ailment. Yet, in his report of the conversation that followed between us, which he gave practically verbatim, I had not expressed a single word of surprise and sorrow at this dreadful intelligence, which to an affectionate husband would be absolutely overwhelming. As it had been proved by the evidence of the nurse and elsewhere that my relations with my young wife were those of deep affection, this struck him as a circumstance so peculiar that he was inclined to think that in this particular Sir John's memory must be at fault.

There was, however, a wide difference between assuming that a portion of the conversation had escaped a witness's memory and disbelieving all that witness's evidence. As the counsel for the Crown had said, if he had not, as he swore, warned me, and I had not, as he swore, refused to listen to his warning, then Sir John Bell was a moral monster. That he, Sir John, at the beginning of my career in Dunchester had shown some prejudice and animus against me was indeed admitted. Doubtless, being human, he was not pleased at the advent of a brilliant young rival, who very shortly proceeded to prove him in the wrong in the instance of one of his own patients, but that he had conquered this feeling, as a man of generous impulses would naturally do, appeared to be clear from the fact that he had volunteered to attend upon that rival's wife in her illness.

From all these facts the jury would draw what inferences seemed just to them, but he for one found it difficult to ask them to include among these the inference that a man who for more than a generation had occupied a very high position among them, whose reputation, both in and out of his profession, was great, and who had received a special mark of favour from the Crown, was in truth an evil-minded and most malevolent perjurer. Yet, if the statement of the accused was to be accepted, that would appear to be the case. Of course, however, there remained the possibility that in the confusion of a hurried interview I might have misunderstood Sir John Bell's words, or that he might have misunderstood mine, or, lastly, as had been suggested, that having come to the conclusion that Sir John could not possibly form a trustworthy opinion on the nature of my wife's symptoms without awaiting their further development, I had determined to neglect advice, in which, as a doctor myself, I had no confidence.

This was the gist of his summing up, but, of course, there was a great deal more which I have not set down. The jury, wishing to consider their verdict, retired, an example that was followed by the judge His departure was the signal for an outburst of conversation in the crowded court, which hummed like a hive of startled bees. The superintendent of police, who, I imagine, had his own opinion of Sir John Bell and of the value of his evidence, very kindly placed a chair for me in the dock, and there on that bad eminence I sat to be studied by a thousand curious and for the most part unsympathetic eyes. Lady Colford had been very popular. Her husband and relations, who were convinced of my guilt and sought to be avenged upon me, were very powerful, therefore the fashionable world of Dunchester, which was doctored by Sir John Bell, was against me almost to a woman.

The jury were long in coming back, and in time I accustomed myself to the staring and comments, and began to think out the problem of my position. It was clear to me that, so far as my future was concerned, it did not matter what verdict the jury gave. In any case I was a ruined man in this and probably in every other country. And there, opposite to me, sat the villain who with no excuse of hot blood or the pressure of sudden passion, had deliberately sworn away my honour and livelihood. He was chatting easily to one of the counsel for the Crown, when presently he met my eyes and in them read my thoughts. I suppose that the man had a conscience somewhere; probably, indeed, his treatment of me had not been premeditated, but was undertaken in a hurry to save himself from well-merited attack. The lie once told there was no escape for him, who henceforth must sound iniquity to its depths.

Suddenly, in the midst of his conversation, Sir John became silent and his lips turned pale and trembled; then, remarking abruptly that he could waste no more time on this miserable business, he rose and left the court. Evidently the barrister to whom he was talking had observed to what this change of demeanour was due, for he looked first at me in the dock and next at Sir John Bell as, recovering his pomposity, he made his way through the crowd. Then he grew reflective, and pushing his wig back from his forehead he stared at the ceiling and whistled to himself softly.

It was very evident that the jury found a difficulty in making up their minds, for minute after minute went by and still they did not return. Indeed, they must have been absent quite an hour and a half when suddenly the superintendent of police removed the chair which he had given me and informed me that "they" were coming.

With a curious and impersonal emotion, as a man might consider a case in which he had no immediate concern, I studied their faces while one by one they filed into the box. The anxiety had been so great and so prolonged that I rejoiced it was at length coming to its end, whatever that end might be.

The judge having returned to his seat on the bench, in the midst of the most intense silence the clerk asked the jury whether they found the prisoner guilty or not guilty. Rising to his feet, the foreman, a dapper little man with a rapid utterance, said, or rather read from a piece of paper, "Not guilty, but we hope that in future Dr. Therne will be more careful about conveying infection."

"That is a most improper verdict," broke in the judge with irritation, "for it acquits the accused and yet implies that he is guilty. Dr. Therne, you are discharged. I repeat that I regret that the jury should have thought fit to add a very uncalled-for rider to their verdict."

I left the dock and pushed my way through the crowd. Outside the court-house I came face to face with Sir Thomas Colford. A sudden impulse moved me to speak to him.

"Sir Thomas," I began, "now that I have been acquitted by a jury—"

"Pray, Dr. Therne," he broke in, "say no more, for the less said the better. It is useless to offer explanations to a man whose wife you have murdered."

"But, Sir Thomas, that is false. When I visited Lady Colford I knew nothing of my wife's condition."

"Sir," he replied, "in this matter I have to choose between the word of Sir John Bell, who, although unfortunately my wife did not like him as a doctor, has been my friend for over twenty years, and your word, with whom I have been acquainted for one year. Under these circumstances, I believe Sir John Bell, and that you are a guilty man. Nine people out of every ten in Dunchester believe this, and, what is more, the jury believed it also, although for reasons which are easily to be understood they showed mercy to you," and, turning on his heel, he walked away from me.

I also walked away to my own desolate home, and, sitting down in the empty consulting-room, contemplated the utter ruin that had overtaken me. My wife was gone and my career was gone, and to whatever part of the earth I might migrate an evil reputation would follow me. And all this through no fault of mine.

Whilst I still sat brooding a man was shown into the room, a smiling little black-coated person, in whom I recognised the managing clerk of the firm of solicitors that had conducted the case for the prosecution.

"Not done with your troubles yet, Dr. Therne, I fear," he said cheerfully; "out of the criminal wood into the civil swamp," and he laughed as he handed me a paper.

"What is this?" I asked.

"Statement of claim in the case of Colford v. Therne; damages laid at 10,000 pounds, which, I daresay, you will agree is not too much for the loss of a young wife. You see, doctor, Sir Thomas is downright wild with you, and so are all the late lady's people. As he can't lock you up, he intends to ruin you by means of an action. If he had listened to me, that is what he would have begun with, leaving the criminal law alone. It's a nasty treacherous thing is the criminal law, and you can't be sure of your man however black things may look against him. I never thought they could convict you, doctor, never; for, as the old judge said, you see it is quite unusual to prosecute criminally in cases of this nature, and the jury won't send a man to jail for a little mistake of the sort. But they will 'cop' you in damages, a thousand or fifteen hundred, and then the best thing that you can do will be to go bankrupt, or perhaps you had better clear before the trial comes on."

I groaned aloud, but the little man went on cheerfully:—

"Same solicitors, I suppose? I'll take the other things to them so as not to bother you more than I can help. Good-afternoon; I'm downright glad that they didn't convict you, and as for old Bell, he's as mad as a hatter, though of course everybody knows what the jury meant—the judge was pretty straight about it, wasn't he?—he chooses to think that it amounts to calling him a liar. Well, now I come to think of it, there are one or two things—so perhaps he is. Good-afternoon, doctor. Let's see, you have the original and I will take the duplicate," and he vanished.

When the clerk had gone I went on thinking. Things were worse than I had believed, for it seemed that I was not even clear of my legal troubles. Already this trial had cost me a great deal, and I was in no position to stand the financial strain of a second appearance in the law courts. Also the man was right; although I had been acquitted on the criminal charge, if the same evidence were given by Sir John Bell and the nurse in a civil action, without any manner of doubt I should be cast in heavy damages. Well, I could only wait and see what happened.

But was it worth while? Was anything worth while? The world had treated me very cruelly; a villain had lied away my reputation and the world believed him, so that henceforth I must be one of its outcasts and black sheep; an object of pity and contempt among the members of my profession. It was doubtful whether, having been thus exposed and made bankrupt, I could ever again obtain a respectable practice. Indeed, the most that I might hope for would be some small appointment on the west coast of Africa, or any other poisonous place, which no one else would be inclined to accept, where I might live—until I died.

The question that occurred to me that evening was whether it would not be wiser on the whole to accept defeat, own myself beaten, and ring down the curtain—not a difficult matter for a doctor to deal with. The arguments for such a course were patent; what were those against it?

The existence of my child? Well, by the time that she grew up, if she lived to grow up, all the trouble and scandal would be forgotten, and the effacement of a discredited parent could be no great loss to her. Moreover, my life was insured for 3000 pounds in an office that took the risk of suicide.

Considerations of religion? These had ceased to have any weight with me. I was brought up to believe in a good and watching Providence, but the events of the last few months had choked that belief. If there was a God who guarded us, why should He have allowed the existence of my wife to be sacrificed to the carelessness, and all my hopes to the villainy, of Sir John Bell? The reasoning was inconclusive, perhaps—for who can know the ends of the Divinity?—but it satisfied my mind at the time, and for the rest I have never really troubled to reopen the question.

The natural love of life for its own sake? It had left me. What more had life to offer? Further, what is called "love of life" frequently enough is little more than fear of the hereafter or of death, and of the physical act of death I had lost my terror, shattered as I was by sorrow and shame. Indeed, at that moment I could have welcomed it gladly, since to me it meant the perfect rest of oblivion.

So in the end I determined that I would leave this lighted house of Life and go out into the dark night, and at once. Unhappy was it for me and for hundreds of other human beings that the decree of fate, or chance, brought my designs to nothing.

First I wrote a letter to be handed to the reporters at the inquest for publication in the newspapers, in which I told the true story of Lady Colford's case and denounced Bell as a villain whose perjury had driven me to self-murder. After this I wrote a second letter, to be given to my daughter if she lived to come to years of discretion, setting out the facts that brought me to my end and asking her to pardon me for having left her. This done it seemed that my worldly business was completed, so I set about leaving the world.

Going to a medicine chest I reflected a little. Finally I decided on prussic acid; its after effects are unpleasant but its action is swift and certain. What did it matter to me if I turned black and smelt of almonds when I was dead?

CHAPTER VI

THE GATE OF DARKNESS

Taking the phial from the chest I poured an ample but not an over dose of the poison into a medicine glass, mixing it with a little water, so that it might be easier to swallow. I lingered as long as I could over these preparations, but they came to an end too soon.

Now there seemed to be nothing more to do except to transfer that little measure of white fluid from the glass to my mouth, and thus to open the great door at whose bolts and bars we stare blankly from the day of birth to the day of death. Every panel of that door is painted with a different picture touched to individual taste. Some are beautiful, and some are grim, and some are neutral-tinted and indefinite. My favourite picture used to be one of a boat floating on a misty ocean, and in the boat a man sleeping—myself, dreaming happily, dreaming always.

But that picture had gone now, and in place of it was one of blackness, not the tumultuous gloom of a stormy night, but dead, cold, unfathomable blackness. Without a doubt that was what lay behind the door—only that. So soon as ever my wine was swallowed and those mighty hinges began to turn I should see a wall of blackness thrusting itself 'twixt door and lintel. Yes, it would creep forward, now pausing, now advancing, until at length it wrapped me round and stifled out my breath like a death mask of cold clay. Then sight would die and sound would die and to all eternities there would be silence, silence while the stars grew old and crumbled, silence while they took form again far in the void, for ever and for ever dumb, dreadful, conquering silence.

That was the only real picture, the rest were mere efforts of the imagination. And yet, what if some of them were also true? What if the finished landscape that lay beyond the doom-door was but developed from the faint sketch traced by the strivings of our spirit—to each man his own picture, but filled in, perfected, vivified a thousandfold, for terror or for joy perfect and inconceivable?

The thought was fascinating, but not without its fears. It was strange that a man who had abandoned hopes should still be haunted by fears—like everything else in the world, this is unjust. For a little while, five or ten minutes, not more than ten, I would let my mind dwell on that thought, trying to dig down to its roots which doubtless drew their strength from the foetid slime of human superstition, trying to behold its topmost branches where they waved in sparkling light. No, that was not the theory; I must imagine those invisible branches as grim skeletons of whitened wood, standing stirless in that atmosphere of overwhelming night.

So I sat myself in a chair, placing the medicine glass with the draught of bane upon the table before me, and, to make sure that I did not exceed the ten minutes, near to it my travelling clock. As I sat thus I fell into a dream or vision. I seemed to see myself standing upon the world, surrounded by familiar sights and sounds. There in the west the sun sank in splendour, and the sails of a windmill that turned slowly between its orb and me were now bright as gold, and now by contrast black as they dipped into the shadow. Near the windmill was a cornfield, and beyond the cornfield stood a cottage whence came the sound of lowing cattle and the voices of children. Down a path that ran through the ripening corn walked a young man and a maid, their arms twined about each other, while above their heads a lark poured out its song.

But at my very feet this kindly earth and all that has life upon it vanished quite away, and there in its place, seen through a giant portal, was the realm of darkness that I had pictured—darkness so terrible, so overpowering, and so icy that my living blood froze at the sight of it. Presently something stirred in the darkness, for it trembled like shaken water. A shape came forward to the edge of the gateway so that the light of the setting sun fell upon it, making it visible. I looked and knew that it was the phantom of my lost wife wrapped in her last garments. There she stood, sad and eager-faced, with quick-moving lips, from which no echo reached my ears. There she stood, beating the air with her hands as though to bar that path against me. . . .

I awoke with a start, to see standing over against me in the gloom of the doorway, not the figure of my wife come from the company of the dead with warning on her lips, but that of Stephen Strong. Yes, it was he, for the light of the candle that I had lit when I went to seek the drug fell full upon his pale face and large bald head.

"Hullo, doctor," he said in his harsh but not unkindly voice, "having a nip and a nap, eh? What's your tipple? Hollands it looks, but it smells more like peach brandy. May I taste it? I'm a judge of hollands," and he lifted the glass of prussic acid and water from the table.

In an instant my dazed faculties were awake, and with a swift motion I had knocked the glass from his hand, so that it fell upon the floor and was shattered.

"Ah!" he said, "I thought so. And now, young man, perhaps you will tell me why you were playing a trick like that?"

"Why?" I answered bitterly. "Because my wife is dead; because my name is disgraced; because my career is ruined; because they have commenced a new action against me, and, if I live, I must become a bankrupt—"

"And you thought that you could make all these things better by killing yourself. Doctor, I didn't believe that you were such a fool. You say you have done nothing to be ashamed of, and I believe you. Well, then, what does it matter what these folk think? For the rest, when a man finds himself in a tight place, he shouldn't knock under, he should fight his way through. You're in a tight place, I know, but I was once in a tighter, yes, I did what you have nearly done—I went to jail on a false charge and false evidence. But I didn't commit suicide. I served my time, and I think it crazed me a bit though it was only a month; at any rate, I was what they call a crank when I came out, which I wasn't when I went in. Then I set to work and showed up those for whom I had done time—living or dead they'll never forget Stephen Strong, I'll warrant—and after that I turned to and became the head of the Radical party and one of the richest men in Dunchester; why, I might have been in Parliament half a dozen times over if I had chosen, although I am only a draper. Now, if I have done all this, why can't you, who have twice my brains and education, do as much?

"Nobody will employ you? I will find folk who will employ you. Action for damages? I'll stand the shot of that however it goes; I love a lawsuit, and a thousand or two won't hurt me. And now I came round here to ask you to supper, and I think you'll be better drinking port with Stephen Strong than hell-fire with another tradesman, whom I won't name. Before we go, however, just give me your word of honour that there shall be no more of this sort of thing," and he pointed to the broken glass, "now or afterwards, as I don't want to be mixed up with inquests."

"I promise," I answered presently.

"That will do," said Mr. Strong, as he led the way to the door.

I need not dwell upon the further events of that evening, inasmuch as they were almost a repetition of those of the previous night. Mrs. Strong received me kindly in her faded fashion, and, after a few inquiries about the trial, sought refuge in her favourite topic of the lost Tribes. Indeed, I remember that she was rather put out because I had not already mastered the books and pamphlets which she had given me. In the end, notwithstanding the weariness of her feeble folly, I returned home in much better spirits.

For the next month or two nothing of note happened to me, except indeed that the action for damages brought against me by Sir Thomas Colford was suddenly withdrawn. Although it never transpired publicly, I believe that the true reason of this collapse was that Sir John Bell flatly refused to appear in court and submit himself to further examination, and without Sir John Bell there was no evidence against me. But the withdrawal of this action did not help me professionally; indeed the fine practice which I was beginning to get together had entirely vanished away. Not a creature came near my consulting-room, and scarcely a creature called me in. The prosecution and the verdict of the jury, amounting as it did to one of "not proven" only, had ruined me. By now my small resources were almost exhausted, and I could see that very shortly the time would come when I should no longer know where to turn for bread for myself and my child.

One morning as I was sitting in my consulting-room, moodily reading a medical textbook for want of something else to do, the front door bell rang. "A patient at last," I thought to myself with a glow of hope. I was soon undeceived, however, for the servant opened the door and announced Mr. Stephen Strong.

"How do you do, doctor?" he said briskly. "You will wonder why I am here at such an hour. Well, it is on business. I want you to come with me to see two sick children."

"Certainly," I said, and we started.

"Who are the children and what is the matter with them?" I asked presently.

"Son and daughter of a working boot-maker named Samuels. As to what is the matter with them, you can judge of that for yourself," he replied with a grim smile.

Passing into the poorer part of the city, at length we reached a cobbler's shop with a few pairs of roughly-made boots on sale in the window. In the shop sat Mr. Samuels, a dour-looking man of about forty.

"Here is the doctor, Samuels," said Strong.

"All right," he answered, "he'll find the missus and the kids in there and a pretty sight they are; I can't bear to look at them, I can't."

Passing through the shop, we went into a back room whence came a sound of wailing. Standing in the room was a careworn woman and in the bed lay two children, aged three and four respectively. I proceeded at once to my examination, and found that one child, a boy, was in a state of extreme prostration and fever, the greater part of his body being covered with a vivid scarlet rash. The other child, a girl, was suffering from a terribly red and swollen arm, the inflammation being most marked above the elbow. Both were cases of palpable and severe erysipelas, and both of the sufferers had been vaccinated within five days.

"Well," said Stephen Strong, "well, what's the matter with them?"

"Erysipelas," I answered.

"And what caused the erysipelas? Was it the vaccination?"

"It may have been the vaccination," I replied cautiously.

"Come here, Samuels," called Strong. "Now, then, tell the doctor your story."

"There's precious little story about it," said the poor man, keeping his back towards the afflicted children. "I have been pulled up three times and fined because I didn't have the kids vaccinated, not being any believer in vaccination myself ever since my sister's boy died of it, with his head all covered with sores. Well, I couldn't pay no more fines, so I told the missus that she might take them to the vaccination officer, and she did five or six days ago. And there, that's the end of their vaccination, and damn 'em to hell, say I," and the poor fellow pushed his way out of the room.

It is quite unnecessary that I should follow all the details of this sad case. In the result, despite everything that I could do for him, the boy died though the girl recovered. Both had been vaccinated from the same tube of lymph. In the end I was able to force the authorities to have the contents of tubes obtained from the same source examined microscopically and subjected to the culture test. They were proved to contain the streptococcus or germ of erysipelas.

As may be imagined this case caused a great stir and much public controversy, in which I took an active part. It was seized upon eagerly by the anti-vaccination party, and I was quoted as the authority for its details. In reply, the other side hinted pretty broadly that I was a person so discredited that my testimony on this or any other matter should be accepted with caution, an unjust aspersion which not unnaturally did much to keep me in the enemy's camp. Indeed it was now, when I became useful to a great and rising party, that at length I found friends without number, who, not content with giving me their present support, took up the case on account of which I had stood my trial, and, by their energy and the ventilation of its details, did much to show how greatly I had been wronged. I did not and do not suppose that all this friendship was disinterested, but, whatever its motive, it was equally welcome to a crushed and deserted man.

By slow degrees, and without my making any distinct pronouncement on the subject, I came to be looked upon as a leading light among the very small and select band of anti-vaccinationist men, and as such to study the question exhaustively. Hearing that I was thus engaged, Stephen Strong offered me a handsome salary, which I suppose came out of his pocket, if I would consent to investigate cases in which vaccination was alleged to have resulted in mischief. I accepted the salary since, formally at any rate, it bound me to nothing but a course of inquiries. During a search of two years I established to my satisfaction that vaccination, as for the most part it was then performed, that is from arm to arm, is occasionally the cause of blood poisoning, erysipelas, abscesses, tuberculosis, and other dreadful ailments. These cases I published without drawing from them any deductions whatever, with the result that I found myself summoned to give evidence before the Royal Commission on Vaccination which was then sitting at Westminster. When I had given my evidence, which, each case being well established, could scarcely be shaken, some members of the Commission attempted to draw me into general statements as to the advantage or otherwise of the practice of vaccination to the community. To these gentlemen I replied that as my studies had been directed towards the effects of vaccination in individual instances only, the argument was one upon which I preferred not to enter.

Had I spoken the truth, indeed, I should have confessed my inability to support the anti-vaccinationist case, since in my opinion few people who have studied this question with an open and impartial mind can deny that Jenner's discovery is one of the greatest boons—perhaps, after the introduction of antiseptics and anaesthetics, the very greatest—that has ever been bestowed upon suffering humanity.

If the reader has any doubts upon the point, let him imagine a time when, as used to happen in the days of our forefathers, almost everybody suffered from smallpox at some period of their lives, those escaping only whose blood was so fortified by nature that the disease could not touch them. Let him imagine a state of affairs—and there are still people living whose parents could remember it—when for a woman not to be pitted with smallpox was to give her some claim to beauty, however homely might be her features. Lastly, let him imagine what all this means: what terror walked abroad when it was common for smallpox to strike a family of children, and when the parents, themselves the survivors of similar catastrophes, knew well that before it left the house it would take its tithe of those beloved lives. Let him look at the brasses in our old churches and among the numbers of children represented on them as kneeling behind their parents; let him note what a large proportion pray with their hands open. Of these, the most, I believe, were cut off by smallpox. Let him search the registers, and they will tell the same tale. Let him ask old people of what their mothers told them when they were young of the working of this pestilence in their youth. Finally, let him consider how it comes about, if vaccination is a fraud, that some nine hundred and ninety-nine medical men out of every thousand, not in England only, but in all civilised countries, place so firm a belief in its virtue. Are the doctors of the world all mad, or all engaged in a great conspiracy to suppress the truth?

These were my real views, as they must be the views of most intelligent and thoughtful men; but I did not think it necessary to promulgate them abroad, since to do so would have been to deprive myself of such means of maintenance as remained to me. Indeed, in those days I told neither more nor less than the truth. Evil results occasionally followed the use of bad lymph or unclean treatment after the subject had been inoculated. Thus most of the cases of erysipelas into which I examined arose not from vaccination but from the dirty surroundings of the patient. Wound a million children, however slightly, and let flies settle on the wound or dirt accumulate in it, and the result will be that a certain small proportion will develop erysipelas quite independently of the effects of vaccination.

In the same way, some amount of inoculated disease must follow the almost promiscuous use of lymph taken from human beings. The danger is perfectly preventable, and ought long ago to have been prevented, by making it illegal, under heavy penalties, to use any substance except that which has been developed in calves and scientifically treated with glycerine, when, as I believe, no hurt can possibly follow. This is the verdict of science and, as tens of thousands can testify, the common experience of mankind.

CHAPTER VII

CROSSING THE RUBICON

My appearance as an expert before the Royal Commission gave me considerable importance in the eyes of a large section of the inhabitants of Dunchester. It was not the wealthiest or most influential section indeed, although in it were numbered some rich and powerful men. Once again I found myself with a wide and rapidly increasing practice, and an income that was sufficient for my needs. Mankind suffers from many ailments besides that of smallpox, indeed in Dunchester this question of the value of vaccination was at that time purely academical, as except for an occasional case there had been no outbreak of smallpox for years. Now, as I have said, I was a master of my trade, and soon proved myself competent to deal skilfully with such illnesses, surgical or medical, as I was called upon to treat. Thus my practice grew, especially among the small tradespeople and artisans, who did not belong to clubs, but preferred to pay for a doctor in whom they had confidence.

Three years and more had gone by since that night on which I sat opposite to a wine-glass full of poison and was the prey of visions, when once again I received a call from Stephen Strong. With this good-hearted, though misguided man, and his amiable, but weak-minded wife, I had kept up an intimacy that in time ripened into genuine friendship. On every Sunday night, and sometimes oftener, I took supper with them, and discussed with Mrs. Strong the important questions of our descent from the lost Tribes and whether or no the lupus from which she suffered was the result of vaccination in infancy.

Owing to a press of patients, to whom I was obliged to attend, I was not able to receive Mr. Strong for nearly half an hour.

"Things are a bit different from what they used to be, doctor," he said as he entered the room looking much the same as ever, with the exception that now even his last hairs had gone, leaving him completely bald, "there's six more of them waiting there, and all except one can pay a fee. Yes, the luck has turned for you since you were called in to attend cobbler Samuels' children, and you haven't seen the top of it yet, I can tell you. Now, what do you think I have come to see you about?"

"Can't say. I give it up."

"Then I will tell you. You saw in yesterday's paper that old brewer Hicks, the member for Dunchester, has been raised to the peerage. I understand he told the Government that if they kept him waiting any longer he would stop his subscription to the party funds, and as that's 5000 pounds a year, they gave in, believing the seat to be a safe one. But that's just where they make their mistake, for if we get the right man the Rads will win."

"And who is the right man?"

"James Therne, Esq., M.D.," he answered quietly.

"What on earth do you mean?" I asked. "How can I afford to spend from 1000 to 2000 pounds upon a contested election, and as much more a year in subscriptions and keeping up the position if I should chance to be returned? And how, in the name of fortune, can I be both a practising physician and a member of Parliament?"

"I'll tell you, doctor, for, ever since your name was put forward by the Liberal Council yesterday, I have seen these difficulties and been thinking them out. Look here, you are still young, handsome, clever, and a capital speaker with a popular audience. Also you are very hard-working and would rise. But you've no money, and only what you earn at your profession to live on, which, if you were a member of Parliament, you couldn't continue to earn. Well, such a man as you are is wanted and so he must be paid for."

"No, no," I said, "I am not going to be the slave of a Radical Five Hundred, bound to do what they tell me and vote as they like; I'd rather stick to my own trade, thank you."

"Don't you be in a hurry, young man; who asked you to be any one's slave? Now, look here—if somebody guarantees every farthing of expense to fight the seat, and 1200 pounds a year and outgoings if you should be successful, and a bonus of 5000 pounds in the event of your being subsequently defeated or electing to give up parliamentary life, will you take on the job?"

"On those terms, yes, I think so, provided I was sure of the guarantor, and that he was a man from whom I could take the money."

"Well, you can soon judge of that, doctor, for it is I, Samuel Strong, and I'll deposit 10,000 pounds in the hands of a trustee before you write your letter of acceptance. No, don't thank me. I do it for two reasons—first, because, having no chick or kin of my own, I happen to have taken a fancy to you and wish to push you on. The world has treated you badly, and I want to see you one of its masters, with all these smart people who look down on you licking your boots, as they will sure enough if you grow rich and powerful. That's my private reason. My public one is that you are the only man in Dunchester who can win us the seat, and I'd think 10,000 pounds well spent if it put those Tories at the bottom of the poll. I want to show them who is "boss," and that we won't be lorded over by bankers and brewers just because they are rich men who have bought themselves titles."

"But you are a rich man yourself," I interrupted.

"Yes, doctor, and I spend my money in helping those who will help the people. Now, before you give me any answer, I've got to ask you a thing or two," and he drew a paper from his pocket. "Are you prepared to support the abolition of 'tied' houses?"

"Certainly. They are the worst monopoly in England."

"Graduated income-tax?"

"Yes; the individual should pay in proportion to the property protected."

"An Old Age Pension scheme?"

"Yes, but only by means of compulsory insurance applicable to all classes without exception."

"Disestablishment and Disendowment of the Church?"

"Yes, provided its funds are pooled and reapplied to Church purposes."

"Payment of members and placing the cost of elections on the rates?"

"Yes, the door of Parliament should not be shut in the face of all except the very rich. Election expenditure is at present only a veiled form of corruption. If it were put upon the rates it could be reduced by at least a half, and elections would be fewer."

"Home Rule—no, I needn't ask you that, for it is a dead horse which we don't want to flog, and now-a-days we are all in favour of a big navy, so I think that is about everything—except, of course, anti-vaccination, which you'll run for all it's worth."

"I never said that I would, Mr. Strong," I answered.

He looked at me curiously. "No, and you never said you wouldn't. Now, doctor, let us come to an understanding about this, for here in Dunchester it's worth more than all the other things put together. If this seat is to be won, it will be won on anti-vaccination. That's our burning question, and that's why you are being asked to stand, because you've studied the thing and are believed to be one of the few doctors who don't bow the knee to Baal. So look here, let's understand each other. If you have any doubts about this matter, say so, and we will have done with it, for, remember, once you are on the platform you've got to go the whole hog; none of your scientific finicking, but appeals to the people to rise up in their thousands and save their innocent children from being offered to the Moloch of vaccination, with enlarged photographs of nasty-looking cases, and the rest of it."

I listened and shivered. The inquiry into rare cases of disease after vaccination had been interesting work, which, whatever deductions people might choose to draw, in fact committed me to nothing. But to become one of the ragged little regiment of medical dissenters, to swallow all the unscientific follies of the anti-vaccination agitators, to make myself responsible for and to promulgate their distorted figures and wild statements—ah! that was another thing. Must I appear upon platforms and denounce this wonderful discovery as the "law of useless infanticide"? Must I tell people that "smallpox is really a curative process and not the deadly scourge and pestilence that doctors pretend it to be"? Must I maintain "that vaccination never did, never does, and never can prevent even a single case of smallpox"? Must I hold it up as a "law (!) of devil worship and human sacrifice to idols"?

If I accepted Strong's offer it seemed that I must do all these things: more, I must be false to my instincts, false to my training and profession, false to my scientific knowledge. I could not do it. And yet—when did a man in my position ever get such a chance as that which was offered to me this day? I was ready with my tongue and fond of public speaking; from boyhood it had been my desire to enter Parliament, where I knew well that I should show to some advantage. Now, without risk or expense to myself, an opportunity of gratifying this ambition was given to me. Indeed, if I succeeded in winning this city, which had always been a Tory stronghold, for the Radical party I should be a marked man from the beginning, and if my career was not one of assured prosperity the fault would be my own. Already in imagination I saw myself rich (for in this way or in that the money would come), a favourite of the people, a trusted minister of the Crown and perhaps—who could tell?—ennobled, living a life of dignity and repute, and at last leaving my honours and my fame to those who came after me.

On the other hand, if I refused this offer the chance would pass away from me, never to return again; it was probable even that I should lose Stephen Strong's friendship and support, for he was not a man who liked his generosity to be slighted, moreover he would believe me unsound upon his favourite dogmas. In short, for ever abandoning my brilliant hopes I condemned myself to an experience of struggle as a doctor with a practice among second-class people.

After all, although the thought of it shocked me at first, the price I was asked to pay was not so very heavy, merely one of the usual election platform formulas, whereby the candidate binds himself to support all sorts of things in which he has little or no beliefs. Already I was half committed to this anti-vaccination crusade, and, if I took a step or two farther in it, what did it matter? One crank more added to the great army of British enthusiasts could make little difference in the scheme of things.

If ever a man went through a "psychological moment" in this hour I was that man. The struggle was short and sharp, but it ended as might be expected in the case of one of my history and character. Could

I have foreseen the dreadful issues which hung upon my decision, I believe that rather than speak it, for the second time in my life I would have sought the solace to be found in the phials of my medicine chest. But I did not foresee them, I thought only of myself, of my own hopes, fears and ambitions, forgetting that no man can live to himself alone, and that his every deed must act and re-act upon others until humanity ceases to exist.

"Well," said Mr. Strong after a two or three minutes' pause, during which these thoughts were wrestling in my mind.

"Well," I answered, "as you elegantly express it, I am prepared to go the whole hog—it is a case of hog versus calf, isn't it?—or, for the matter of that, a whole styful of hogs."

I suppose that my doubts and irritation were apparent in the inelegant jocosity of my manner. At any rate, Stephen Strong, who was a shrewd observer, took alarm.

"Look here, doctor," he said, "I am honest, I am; right or wrong I believe in this anti-vaccination business, and we are going to run the election on it. If you don't believe in it—and you have no particular call to, since every man can claim his own opinion—you'd better let it alone, and look on all this talk as nothing. You are our first and best man, but we have several upon the list; I'll go on to one of them," and he took up his hat.

I let him take it; I even let him walk towards the door; but, as he approached it, I reflected that with that dogged burly form went all my ambitions and my last chance of advancement in life. When his hand was already on the handle, not of premeditation, but by impulse, I said:—

"I don't know why you should talk like that, as I think that I have given good proof that I am no believer in vaccination."

"What's that, doctor?" he asked turning round.

"My little girl is nearly four years old and she has never been vaccinated."

"Is it so?" he asked doubtfully.

As he spoke I heard the nurse going down the passage and with her my daughter, whom she was taking for her morning walk. I opened the door and called Jane in, a beautiful little being with dark eyes and golden hair.

"Look for yourself," I said, and, taking off the child's coat, I showed him both her arms. Then I kissed her and sent her back to the nurse.

"That's good enough, doctor, but, mind you, she mustn't be vaccinated now."

As he spoke the words my heart sank in me, for I understood what I had done and the risk that I was taking. But the die was cast, or so I thought, in my folly. It was too late to go back.

"Don't be afraid," I said, "no cow poison shall be mixed with her blood."

"Now I believe you, doctor," he answered, "for a man won't play tricks with his only child just to help himself. I'll take your answer to the council, and they will send you the formal letter of invitation to stand with the conditions attached. Before you answer it the money will be lodged, and you shall have my bond for it. And now I must be going, for I am wasting your time and those patients of yours will be getting tired. If you will come to supper to-night I'll have some of the leaders to meet you and we can talk things over. Good-bye, we shall win the seat; so sure as my name is Stephen Strong we shall win on the A.V. ticket."

He went, and I saw those of my patients who had sat out the wait. When they had gone, I considered the position, summing it up in my own mind. The prospect was exhilarating, and yet I was depressed, for I had bound myself to the chariot wheels of a false doctrine. Also, by implication, I had told Strong a lie. It was true that Jane had not been vaccinated, but of this I had neglected to give him the reason. It was that I had postponed vaccinating her for a while owing to a certain infantile delicacy, being better acquainted than most men with the risks consequent on that operation, slight though it is, in certain conditions of a child's health, and knowing that there was no danger of her taking smallpox in a town which was free from it. I proposed, however, to perform the operation within the next few days; indeed, for this very purpose I had already written to London to secure some glycerinated calf lymph, which would now be wasted.

The local papers next morning appeared with an announcement that at the forthcoming bye-election Dunchester would be contested in the Radical interest by James Therne, Esq., M.D. They added that, in addition to other articles of the Radical faith, Dr. Therne professed the doctrine of anti-vaccination, of which he was so ardent an upholder that, although on several occasions he had been threatened with prosecution, he declined to allow his only child to be vaccinated.

In the same issues it was announced that the Conservative candidate would be Sir Thomas Colford.

So the die was cast. I had crossed the Rubicon.

CHAPTER VIII

BRAVO THE A.V.'S

In another week the writ had been issued, and we were in the thick of the fight. What a fight it was! Memory could not record; tradition did not even record another half as fierce in the borough of Dunchester. For the most part, that is in many of our constituencies, it is not difficult for a candidate standing in the Radical interest, if he is able, well-backed, and not too particular as to what he promises, to win the seat for his party. But Dunchester was something of an exception. In a sense it was corrupt, that is, it had always been represented by a rich man, who was expected to pay liberally for the honour of its confidence. Pay he did, indeed, in large and numberless subscriptions, in the endowment of reading-rooms, in presents of public parks, and I know not what besides.

At least it is a fact that almost every advantage of this nature enjoyed to-day by the inhabitants of Dunchester, has been provided for them by former Conservative members for the borough.

Under these circumstances it is not to be wondered at that in choosing a candidate the majority of the electors of the city were apt to ask two leading questions: first, Is he rich? and secondly, What will he do for the town if he gets in?

Now, Sir Thomas Colford was very rich, and it was whispered that if he were elected he would be prepared to show his gratitude in a substantial fashion. A new wing to the hospital was wanted; this it was said would be erected and endowed; also forty acres of valuable land belonging to him ran into the park, and he had been heard to say that these forty acres were really much more important to the public than to himself, and that he hoped that one day they would belong to it.

It is small wonder, then, that the announcement of his candidature was received with passionate enthusiasm. Mine, on the contrary, evoked a chorus of disapproval, that is, in the local press. I was denounced as an adventurer, as a man who had stood a criminal trial for wicked negligence, and escaped the jail only by the skin of my teeth. I was held up to public reprobation as a Socialist, who, having nothing myself, wished to prey upon the goods of others, and as an anti-vaccination quack who, to gain a few votes, was ready to infest the whole community with a loathsome disease. Of all the accusations of my opponents this was the only one that stung me, because it alone had truth in it.

Sir John Bell, my old enemy, one of the nominators of Sir Thomas Colford, appeared upon the platform at his first meeting, and, speaking in the character of an old and leading citizen of the town, and as one who had doctored most of them, implored his audience not to trust their political fortunes to such a person as myself, whose doctrines were repudiated by almost every member of the profession, which I disgraced. This appeal carried much weight with it.

From all these circumstances it might have been supposed that my case was hopeless, especially as no Radical had even ventured to contest the seat in the last two elections. But, in fact, this was not so, for in Dunchester there existed a large body of voters, many of them employed in shoe-making factories, who were almost socialistic in their views. These men, spending their days in some hive of machinery, and their nights in squalid tenements built in dreary rows, which in cities such people are doomed to inhabit, were very bitter against the upper classes, and indeed against all who lived in decent comfort.

This was not to be marvelled at, for what can be expected of folk whose lot, hard as it is, has none of the mitigations that lighten the troubles of those who live in the country, and who can at least breathe the free air and enjoy the beauties that are common to all? Here, at Dunchester, their pleasures consisted for the most part in a dog fight or some such refining spectacle, varied by an occasional "boose" at the public-house, or, in the case of those who chanced to be more intellectually inclined, by attending lectures where Socialism and other advanced doctrines were preached. As was but natural, this class might be relied upon almost to a man to vote for the party which promised to better their lot, rather than for the party which could only recommend them to be contented and to improve themselves. To secure their support it was only necessary to be extravagant of promises and abusive of employers who refused to pay them impossible wages.

Next in importance to these red-hot "forwards" came the phalanx of old-fashioned people who voted Liberal because their fathers had voted Liberal before them. Then there were the electors who used to be Conservative but, being honestly dissatisfied with the Government on account of its foreign policy, or for other reasons, had made up their minds to transfer their allegiance. Also there were the dissenters, who set hatred of the Church above all politics, and made its disendowment and humiliation their watchword. In Dunchester these were active and numerous, a very tower of strength to me, for Stephen Strong was the wealthiest and most important of them.

During the first day or two of the canvass, however, a careful estimate of our electoral strength showed it to be several hundred votes short of that of our opponents. Therefore, if we would win, we must make converts by appealing to the prejudices of members of the electorate who were of Conservative views; in other words, by preaching "fads."

Of these there were many, all useful to the candidate of pliant mind, such as the total drink-prohibition fad, the anti-dog-muzzling fad, and others, each of which was worth some votes. Even the Peculiar People, a society that makes a religion of killing helpless children by refusing them medical aid when they are ill, were good for ten or twelve. Here, however, I drew the line, for when asking whether I would support a bill relieving them from all liability to criminal prosecution in the event of the death of their victims, I absolutely declined to give any such undertaking.

But although all these fancies had their followers, it was the anti-vaccination craze that really had a hold in Dunchester. The "A.V.'s," as they called themselves, were numbered by hundreds, for the National League and other similar associations had been at work here for years, with such success that already twenty per cent. of the children born in the last decade had never been vaccinated. For a while the Board of Guardians had been slow to move, then, on the election of a new chairman and the representations of the medical profession of the town, they instituted a series of prosecutions against parents who refused to comply with the Vaccination Acts. Unluckily for the Conservative party, these prosecutions, which aroused the most bitter feelings, were still going on when the seat fell vacant; hence from an electoral point of view the question became one of first-class importance.

In Dunchester, as elsewhere, the great majority of the anti-vaccinators were already Radical, but there remained a residue, estimated at from 300 to 400, who voted "blue" or Conservative. If these men could be brought over, I should win; if they remained faithful to their colour, I must lose. Therefore it will be seen that Stephen Strong was right when he said that the election would be won or lost upon anti-vaccination.

At the first public meeting of the Conservatives, after Sir Thomas's speech, the spokesman of the anti-vaccination party rose and asked him whether he was in favour of the abolition of the Compulsory Vaccination laws. Now, at this very meeting Sir John Bell had already spoken denouncing me for my views upon this question, thereby to some extent tying the candidate's hands. So, after some pause and consultation, Sir Thomas replied that he was in favour of freeing "Conscientious Objectors" to vaccination from all legal penalties. Like most half measures, this decision of course did not gain him a single vote, whereas it certainly lost him much support.

On the same evening a similar question was put to me. My answer may be guessed, indeed I took the opportunity to make a speech which was cheered to the echo, for, having acted the great lie of espousing the anti-vaccination cause, I felt that it was not worth while to hesitate in telling other lies in support of it. Moreover, I knew my subject thoroughly, and understood what points to dwell upon and what to gloze over, how to twist and turn the statistics, and how to marshal my facts in such fashion as would make it very difficult to expose their fallacy. Then, when I had done with general arguments, I went on to particular cases, describing as a doctor can do the most dreadful which had ever come under my notice, with such power and pathos that women in the audience burst into tears.

Finally, I ended by an impassioned appeal to all present to follow my example and refuse to allow their children to be poisoned. I called on them as free men to rise against this monstrous Tyranny, to put a stop to this system of organised and judicial Infanticide, and to send me to Parliament to raise my voice on their behalf in the cause of helpless infants whose tender bodies now, day by day, under the command of the law, were made the receptacles of the most filthy diseases from which man was doomed to suffer.

As I sat down the whole of that great audience—it numbered more than 2000—rose in their places shouting "We will! we will!" after which followed a scene of enthusiasm such as I had never seen before, emphasised by cries of "We are free Englishmen," "Down with the baby-butchers," "We will put you in, sir," and so forth.

That meeting gave me my cue, and thenceforward, leaving almost every other topic on one side, I and my workers devoted ourselves to preaching the anti-vaccination doctrines. We flooded the constituency with tracts headed "What Vaccination does," "The Law of Useless Infanticide," "The Vaccine Tyranny," "Is Vaccination a Fraud?" and so forth, and with horrible pictures of calves stretched out by pulleys, gagged and blindfolded, with their under parts covered by vaccine vesicles. Also we had photographs of children suffering from the effects of improper or unclean vaccination, which, by means of magic lantern slides, could be thrown life-sized on a screen; indeed, one or two such children themselves were taken round to meetings and their sores exhibited.

The effect of all this was wonderful, for I know of nothing capable of rousing honest but ignorant people to greater rage and enthusiasm than this anti-vaccination cry. They believe it to be true, or, at least, seeing one or two cases in which it is true, and having never seen a case of smallpox, they suppose that the whole race is being poisoned by wicked doctors for their own gain. Hence their fierce energy and heartfelt indignation.

Well, it carried me through. The election was fought not with foils but with rapiers. Against me were arrayed the entire wealth, rank, and fashion of the city, reinforced by Conservative speakers famous for their parliamentary eloquence, who were sent down to support Sir Thomas Colford. Nor was this all: when it was recognised that the fight would be a close one, an eloquent and leading member of the House was sent to intervene in person. He came and addressed a vast meeting gathered in the biggest building of the city. Seated among a crowd of workmen on a back bench I was one of his audience. His speech was excellent, if somewhat too general and academic. To the "A.V." agitation, with a curious misapprehension of the state of the case, he devoted one paragraph only. It ran something like this:—

"I am told that our opponents, putting aside the great and general issues upon which I have had the honour to address you, attempt to gain support by entering upon a crusade—to my mind a most pernicious crusade—against the law of compulsory vaccination. I am not concerned to defend that law, because practically in the mind of all reasonable men it stands beyond attack. It is, I am told, suggested that the Act should be amended by freeing from the usual penalties any parent who chooses to advance a plea of conscientious objection against the vaccination of his children. Such an argument seems to me too puerile, I had almost said too wicked, to dwell upon, for in its issue it would mean that at the whim of individuals innocent children might be exposed to disease, disfigurement, and death, and the whole community through them to a very real and imminent danger. Prophecy is dangerous, but, speaking for myself as a private member of Parliament, I can scarcely believe that responsible ministers of any party, moved by the pressure of an ill-informed and erroneous opinion, would ever consent under this elastic plea of conscience to establish such a precedent of surrender. Vaccination with its proved benefits is outside the pale of party. After long and careful study, science and the medical profession have given a verdict in its favour, a verdict which has now been confirmed by the experience of generations. Here I leave the question, and, turning once more before I sit down to those great and general issues of which I have already spoken, I would again impress upon this vast audience, and through it upon the constituency at large," etc., etc., etc.

Within a year it was my lot to listen to an eminent leader of that distinguished member (with the distinguished member's tacit consent) pressing upon an astonished House of Commons the need of yielding to the clamour of the anti-vaccinationists, and of inserting into the Bill, framed upon the report of a Royal Commission, a clause forbidding the prosecution of parents or guardians willing to assert before a bench of magistrates that they objected to vaccination on conscientious grounds.

The appeal was not in vain; the Bill passed in its amended form; and within twenty years I lived to see its fruits.

At length came the polling day. After this lapse of time I remember little of its details. I, as became a Democratic candidate, walked from polling-station to polling-station, while my opponent, as became a wealthy banker, drove about the city in a carriage and four. At eight o'clock the ballot-boxes were sealed up and conveyed to the town-hall, where the counting commenced in the presence of the Mayor, the candidates, their agents, and the necessary officers and assistants. Box after box was opened and the papers counted out into separate heaps, those for Colford into one pile, those for Therne into another, the spoiled votes being kept by themselves.

The counting began about half-past nine, and up to a quarter to twelve nobody could form an idea as to the ultimate result, although at that time the Conservative candidate appeared to be about five and thirty votes ahead. Then the last ballot-box was opened; it came from a poor quarter of the city, a ward in which I had many supporters.

Sir Thomas Colford and I, with our little knots of agents and sub-agents, placed ourselves one on each side of the table, waiting in respectful silence while the clerk dealt out the papers, as a player deals out cards. It was an anxious moment, as any one who has gone through a closely-contested parliamentary election can testify. For ten days or more the strain had been great, but, curiously enough, now at its climax it seemed to have lost its grip of me. I watched the denoument of the game with keenness and interest indeed, but as though I were not immediately and personally concerned. I felt that I had done my best to win, and no longer cared whether my efforts ended in success or failure. Possibly this was the result of the apathy that falls upon overstrained nerves. Possibly I was oppressed by the fear of victory and of that Nemesis which almost invariably dogs the steps of our accomplished desires, of what the French writer calls la page effrayante . . . des desirs accomplis. At least just then I cared nothing whether I won or lost, only I reflected that in the latter event it would be sad to have told so many falsehoods to no good purpose.

"How does it stand?" asked the head Conservative agent of the officer.

The clerk took the last numbers from the counters and added up the figures.

"Colford, 4303; Therne, 4291, and two more bundles to count."

Another packet was counted out.

"How does it stand?" asked the agent.

"Colford, 4349; Therne, 4327, and one more bundle of fifty to count," answered the clerk.

The agent gave a sigh of relief and smiled; I saw him press Sir Thomas's hand in congratulations, for now he was sure that victory was theirs.

"The game is up," I whispered to Strong, who, as my principal supporter, had been admitted with me to the hall.

He ground his teeth and I noticed in the gaslight that his face was ghastly pale and his lips were blue.

"You had better go out," I said, "you are overtaxing that dilated heart of yours. Go home and take a sleeping draught."

"Damn you, no," he answered fiercely in my ear, "those papers come from the Little Martha ward, where I thought there wasn't a wrong 'un in the crowd. If they've sold me, I'll be even with them, as sure as my name is Strong."

"Come," I said with a laugh, "a good Radical shouldn't talk like that." For me the bitterness was over, and, knowing the worst, I could afford to laugh.

The official opened the last packet and began to count aloud.

The first vote was for "Therne," but bad, for the elector had written his name upon the paper. Then in succession came nine for "Colford." Now all interest in the result had died away, and a hum of talk arose from those present in the room, a whispered murmur of congratulations and condolences. No wonder, seeing that to win I must put to my credit thirty-two of the forty remaining papers, which seemed a thing impossible.

The counter went on counting aloud and dealing down the papers as he counted. One, two, three, four, and straight on up to ten for Therne, when he paused to examine a paper, then "One for Colford." Then, in rapid successful, "Five, ten, fifteen for Therne."

Now the hum of conversation died away, for it was felt that this was becoming interesting. Of course it was practically impossible that I should win, for there were but fourteen papers left, and to do so I must secure eleven of them!

"Sixteen for Therne," went on the counter, "seventeen, eighteen, nineteen, twenty."

Now the excitement grew intense, for if the run held in two more votes I should tie. Every eye was fixed upon the counter's hand.

To the right and left of him on the table were two little piles of voting papers. The pile to the right was the property of Colford, the pile to the left was sacred to Therne. The paper was unfolded and glanced at, then up went the hand and down floated the fateful sheet on to the left-hand pile. "Twenty-one for

Therne." Again the process was repeated, and again the left-hand pile was increased. "Twenty-two for Therne."

"By heaven! you've tied him," gasped Stephen Strong.

There were but seven papers left, and the candidate who secured four of them would be the winner of the election.

"Twenty-three for Therne, twenty-four, twenty-five"—a silence in which you could hear the breath of other men and the beating of your own heart.

"Twenty-six for Therne, twenty-seven, twenty-eight, twenty-nine, all for Therne."

Then, bursting from the lips of Stephen Strong, a shrill hoarse cry, more like the cry of a beast than that of a man, and the words, "By God! we've won. The A.V.'s have done it. Bravo the A.V.'s!"

"Silence!" said the Mayor, bringing his fist down upon the table, but so far as Stephen Strong was concerned, the order was superfluous, for suddenly his face flushed, then turned a dreadful ashen grey, and down he sank upon the floor. As I leant over him and began to loosen his collar, I heard the Conservative agent say in strident tones:—

"There is some mistake, there must be some mistake. It is almost impossible that Dr. Therne can have polled twenty-nine votes in succession. On behalf of Sir Thomas Colford, I demand a recount."

"Certainly," answered some official, "let it be begun at once."

In that ceremony I took no part; indeed, I spent the next two hours, with the help of another doctor, trying to restore consciousness to Stephen Strong in a little room that opened off the town-hall. Within half an hour Mrs. Strong arrived.

"He still breathes," I said in answer to her questioning glance.

Then the poor little woman sat herself down upon the edge of a chair, clasped her hands and said, "If the Lord wills it, dear Stephen will live; and if the Lord wills it, he will die."

This sentence she repeated at intervals until the end came. After two hours there was a knocking at the door.

"Go away," I said, but the knocker would not go away. So I opened. It was my agent, who whispered in an excited voice, "The count's quite correct, you are in by seven."

"All right," I answered, "tell them we want some more brandy."

At that moment Stephen Strong opened his eyes, and at that moment also there arose a mighty burst of cheering from the crowd assembled on the market-place without, to whom the Mayor had declared the numbers from a window of the town-hall.

The dying man heard the cheering, and looked at me inquiringly, for he could not speak. I tried to explain that I was elected on the recount, but was unable to make him understand. Then I hit upon an expedient. On the floor lay a Conservative rosette of blue ribbon. I took it up and took also my own Radical colours from my coat. Holding one of them in each hand before Strong's dying eyes, I lifted up the Radical orange and let the Conservative blue fall to the floor.

He saw and understood, for a ghastly smile appeared upon his distorted face. Indeed, he did more—almost with his last breath he spoke in a hoarse, gurgling whisper, and his words were, "Bravo the A.V.'s!"

Now he shut his eyes, and I thought that the end had come, but, opening them presently, he fixed them with great earnestness first upon myself and then upon his wife, accompanying the glance with a slight movement of the head. I did not know what he could mean, but with his wife it was otherwise, for she said, "Don't trouble yourself, Stephen, I quite understand."

Five minutes more and it was over; Stephen Strong's dilated heart had contracted for the last time.

"I see it has pleased the Lord that dear Stephen should die," said Mrs. Strong in her quiet voice. "When you have spoken to the people out there, doctor, will you take me home? I am very sorry to trouble, but I saw that after he was gone Stephen wished me to turn to you."

CHAPTER IX

FORTUNE

My return to Parliament meant not only the loss of a seat to the Government, a matter of no great moment in view of their enormous majority, but, probably, through their own fears, was construed by them into a solemn warning not to be disregarded. Certain papers and opposition speakers talked freely of the writing on the wall, and none saw that writing in larger, or more fiery letters, than the members of Her Majesty's Government. I believe that to them it took the form not of Hebraic characters, but of two large Roman capitals, the letters A and V.

Hitherto the anti-vaccinators had been known as troublesome people who had to be reckoned with, but that they should prove strong enough to wrest what had been considered one of the safest seats in the kingdom out of the hands of the Unionists came upon the party as a revelation of the most unpleasant order. For Stephen Strong's dying cry, of which the truth was universally acknowledged, "The A.V.'s have done it. Bravo the A.V.'s!" had echoed through the length and breadth of the land.

When a Government thinks that agitators are weak, naturally and properly it treats them with contempt, but, when it finds that they are strong enough to win elections, then their arguments become more worthy of consideration. And so the great heart of the parliamentary Pharaoh began to soften towards the anti-vaccinators, and of this softening the first signs were discernible within three or four days of my taking my seat as member for Dunchester.

I think I may say without vanity, and the statement will not be contradicted by those who sat with me, that I made a good impression upon the House from the first day I entered its doors. Doubtless its members had expected to find in me a rabid person liable to burst into a foam of violence at the word "vaccination," and were agreeably surprised to find that I was much as other men are, only rather quieter than most of them. I did not attempt to force myself upon the notice of the House, but once or twice during the dinner hour I made a few remarks upon subjects connected with public health which were received without impatience, and, in the interval, I tried to master its forms, and to get in touch with its temper.

In those far-away and long-forgotten days a Royal Commission had been sitting for some years to consider the whole question of compulsory vaccination; it was the same before which I had been called to give evidence. At length this commission delivered itself of its final report, a very sensible one in an enormous blue-book, which if adopted would practically have continued the existing Vaccination Acts with amendments. These amendments provided that in future the public vaccinator should visit the home of the child, and, if the conditions of that home and of the child itself were healthy, offer to vaccinate it with glycerinated calf lymph. Also they extended the time during which the parents and guardians were exempt from prosecution, and in various ways mitigated the rigour of the prevailing regulations. The subject matter of this report was embodied in a short Bill to amend the law and laid before Parliament, which Bill went to a standing committee, and ultimately came up for the consideration of the House.

Then followed the great debate and the great surprise. A member moved that it should be read that day six months, and others followed on the same side. The President of the Local Government Board of the day, I remember, made a strong speech in favour of the Bill, after which other members spoke, including myself. But although about ninety out of every hundred of the individuals who then constituted the House of Commons were strong believers in the merits of vaccination, hardly one of them rose in his place to support the Bill. The lesson of Dunchester amongst others was before their eyes, and, whatever their private faith might be, they were convinced that if they did so it would lose them votes at the next election.

At this ominous silence the Government grew frightened, and towards the end of the debate, to the astonishment of the House and of the country, the First Lord of the Treasury rose and offered to insert a clause by virtue of which any parent or other person who under the Bill would be liable to penalties for the non-vaccination of a child, should be entirely freed from such penalties if within four months of its birth he satisfied two justices of the peace that he conscientiously believed that the operation would be prejudicial to that child's health. The Bill passed with the clause, which a few days later was rejected by the House of Lords. Government pressure was put upon the Lords, who thereon reversed their decision, and the Bill became an Act of Parliament.

Thus the whole policy of compulsory vaccination, which for many years had been in force in England, was destroyed at a single blow by a Government with a great majority, and a House of Commons composed of members who, for the most part, were absolute believers in its virtues. Never before did agitators meet with so vast and complete a success, and seldom perhaps did a Government undertake so great a responsibility for the sake of peace, and in order to shelve a troublesome and dangerous dispute. It was a very triumph of opportunism, for the Government, aided and abetted by their supporters, threw over their beliefs to appease a small but persistent section of the electors. Convinced that compulsory vaccination was for the benefit of the community, they yet stretched the theory of the authority of the parent over the child to such an unprecedented extent that, in order to satisfy his individual prejudices, that parent was henceforth to be allowed to expose his helpless infant to the risk of terrible disease and of death.

It is not for me to judge their motives, which may have been pure and excellent; my own are enough for me to deal with. But the fact remains that, having power in their hands to impose the conclusions of a committee of experts on the nation, and being as a body satisfied as to the soundness of those conclusions, they still took the risk of disregarding them. Now the result of their action is evident; now we have reaped the seed which they sowed, nor did they win a vote or a "thank you" by their amiable and philosophic concessions, which earned them no gratitude but indignation mingled with something not unlike contempt.

So much for the anti-vaccination agitation, on the crest of whose wave I was carried to fortune and success. Thenceforward for many long years my career was one of strange and startling prosperity. Dunchester became my pocket borough, so much so, indeed, that at the three elections which occurred before the last of which I have to tell no one even ventured to contest the seat against me. Although I was never recognised as a leader of men, chiefly, I believe, because of a secret distrust which was entertained as to my character and the sincerity of my motives, session by session my parliamentary repute increased, till, in the last Radical Government, I was offered, and for two years filled, the post of Under-Secretary to the Home Office. Indeed, when at last we went to the country over the question of the China War, I had in my pocket a discreetly worded undertaking that, if our party succeeded at the polls, my claims to the Home Secretaryship should be "carefully considered." But it was not fated that I should ever again cross the threshold of St. Stephen's.

So much for my public career, which I have only touched on in illustration of my private and moral history.

The reader may wonder how it came about that I was able to support myself and keep up my position during all this space of time, seeing that my attendance in Parliament made it impossible for me to continue in practise as a doctor. It happened thus.

When my old and true friend, Stephen Strong, died on the night of my election, it was found that he was even richer than had been supposed, indeed his personalty was sworn at 191,000 pounds, besides which he left real estate in shops, houses and land to the value of about 23,000 pounds. Almost all of this was devised to his widow absolutely, so that she could dispose of it in whatever fashion pleased her. Indeed, there was but one other bequest, that of the balance of the 10,000 pounds which the testator had deposited in the hands of a trustee for my benefit. This was now left to me absolutely. I learned the fact from Mrs. Strong herself as we returned from the funeral.

"Dear Stephen has left you nearly 9000 pounds, doctor," she said shaking her head.

Gathering from her manner and this shake of her head that the legacy was not pleasing to her, I hastened to explain that doubtless it was to carry into effect a business arrangement we had come to before I consented to stand for Parliament.

"Ah, indeed," she said, "that makes it worse, for it is only the payment of a debt, not a gift."

Not knowing what she could mean, I said nothing.

"Doubtless, doctor, if dear Stephen had been granted time he would have treated you more liberally, seeing how much he thought of you, and that you had given up your profession entirely to please him and serve the party. That is what he meant when he looked at me before he died, I guessed it from the first, and now I am sure of it. Well, doctor, while I have anything you shall never want. Of course, a member of Parliament is a great person, expected to live in a style which would take more money than I have, but I think that if I put my own expenses at 500 pounds a year, which is as much as I shall want, and allow another 1000 pounds for subscriptions to the anti-vaccination societies, the society for preventing the muzzling of dogs, and the society for the discovery of the lost Tribes of Israel, I shall be able to help you to the extent of 1200 pounds a year, if," she added apologetically, "you think you could possibly get along on that."

"But, Mrs. Strong," I said, "I have no claim at all upon you."

"Please do not talk nonsense, doctor. Dear Stephen wished me to provide for you, and I am only carrying out his wishes with his own money which God gave him perhaps for this very purpose, that it should be used to help a clever man to break down the tyranny of wicked governments and false prophets."

So I took the money, which was paid with the utmost regularity on January the first and June the first in each year. On this income I lived in comfort, keeping up my house in Dunchester for the benefit of my little daughter and her attendants, and hiring for my own use a flat quite close to the House of Commons.

As the years went by, however, a great anxiety took possession of me, for by slow degrees Mrs. Strong grew as feeble in mind as already she was in body, till at length, she could only recognise people at intervals, and became quite incompetent to transact business. For a while her bankers went on paying the allowance under her written and unrevoked order, but when they understood her true condition, they refused to continue the payment.

Now my position was very serious. I had little or nothing put by, and, having ceased to practise for about seventeen years, I could not hope to earn an income from my profession. Nor could I remain a member of the House, at least not for long. Still, by dint of borrowing and the mortgage of some property which I had acquired, I kept my head above water for about eighteen months. Very soon, however, my financial distress became known, with the result that I was no longer so cordially received as I had been either in Dunchester or in London. The impecunious cannot expect to remain popular.

At last things came to a climax, and I was driven to the step of resigning my seat. I was in London at the time, and thence I wrote the letter to the chairman of the Radical committee in Dunchester giving ill-health as the cause of my retirement. When at length it was finished to my satisfaction, I went out and posted it, and then walked along the embankment as far as Cleopatra's Needle and back again. It was a melancholy walk, taken, I remember, upon a melancholy November afternoon, on which the dank mist from the river strove for mastery with the gloomy shadows of advancing night. Not since that other evening, many many years ago, when, after my trial, I found myself face to face with ruin or death and was saved by Stephen Strong had my fortunes been at so low an ebb. Now, indeed, they appeared absolutely hopeless, for I was no longer young and fit to begin the world afresh; also, the other party being in power, I could not hope to obtain any salaried appointment upon which to support myself and my daughter. If Mrs. Strong had kept her reason all would have been well, but she was insane, and I had no one to whom I could turn, for I was a man of many acquaintances but few friends.

Wearily I trudged back to my rooms to wait there until it was time to dress, for I had a dinner engagement at the Reform Club. On the table in the little hall lay a telegram, which I opened listlessly. It was from a well-known firm of solicitors in Dunchester, and ran:—

"Our client, Mrs. Strong, died suddenly at three o'clock. Important that we should see you. Will you be in Dunchester to-morrow? If not, please say where and at what hour we can wait upon you in town."

"Wait upon you in town," I said to myself as I laid down the telegram. A great firm of solicitors would not wish to wait upon me unless they had something to tell me to my advantage and their own. Mrs. Strong must have left me some money. Possibly even I was her heir. More than once before in life my luck had turned in this sudden way, why should it not happen again? But she was insane and could not appoint an heir! Why had not those fools of lawyers told me the facts instead of leaving me to the torment of this suspense?

I glanced at the clock, then taking a telegraph form I wrote: "Shall be at Dunchester Station 8:30. Meet me there or later at the club." Taking a cab I drove to St. Pancras, just in time to catch the train. In my pocket—so closely was I pressed for money, for my account at the bank was actually overdrawn—I had barely enough to pay for a third-class ticket to Dunchester. This mattered little, however, for I always travelled third-class, not because I liked it but because it looked democratic and the right sort of thing for a Radical M.P. to do.

The train was a fast one, but that journey seemed absolutely endless. Now at length we had slowed down at the Dunchester signal-box, and now we were running into the town. If my friend the lawyer had anything really striking to tell me he would send to meet me at the station, and, if it was something remarkable, he would probably attend there himself. Therefore, if I saw neither the managing clerk nor the junior partner, nor the Head of the Firm, I might be certain that the news was trivial, probably—dreadful thought which had not occurred to me before—that I was appointed executor under the will with a legacy of a hundred guineas.

The train rolled into the station. As it began to glide past the pavement of wet asphalt I closed my eyes to postpone the bitterness of disappointment, if only for a few seconds. Perforce I opened them again as the train was stopping, and there, the very first thing they fell upon, looking portly and imposing in a fur coat, was the rubicund-faced Head of the Firm himself. "It is good," I thought, and supported myself for a moment by the hat-rack, for the revulsion of feeling produced a sudden faintness. He saw me, and sprang forward with a beaming yet respectful countenance. "It is very good," I thought.

"My dear sir," he began obsequiously, "I do trust that my telegram has not incommoded you, but my news was such that I felt it necessary to meet you at the earliest possible moment, and therefore wired to you at every probable address."

I gave the porter who took my bag a shilling. Practically it was my last, but that lawyer's face and manner seemed to justify the expenditure which—so oddly are our minds constituted—I remember reflecting I might regret if I had drawn a false inference. The man touched his hat profusely, and, I hope, made up his mind to vote for me next time. Then I turned to the Head of the Firm and said:—

"Pray, don't apologise; but, by the way, beyond that of the death of my poor friend, what is the news?"

"Oh, perhaps you know it," he answered, taken aback at my manner, "though she always insisted upon its being kept a dead secret, so that one day you might have a pleasant surprise."

"I know nothing," I answered.

"Then I am glad to be the bearer of such good intelligence to a fortunate and distinguished man," he said with a bow. "I have the honour to inform you in my capacity of executor to the will of the late Mrs. Martha Strong that, with the exception of a few legacies, you are left her sole heir."

Now I wished that the hat-rack was still at hand, but, as it was not, I pretended to stumble, and leant for a moment against the porter who had received my last shilling.

"Indeed," I said recovering myself, "and can you tell me the amount of the property?"

"Not exactly," he answered, "but she has led a very saving life, and money grows, you know, money grows. I should say it must be between three and four hundred thousand, nearer the latter than the former, perhaps."

"Really," I replied, "that is more than I expected; it is a little astonishing to be lifted in a moment from the position of one with a mere competence into that of a rich man. But our poor friend was—well, weak-minded, so how could she be competent to make a binding will?"

"My dear sir, her will was made within a month of her husband's death, when she was as sane as you are, as I have plenty of letters to show. Only, as I have said, she kept the contents a dead secret, in order that one day they might be a pleasant surprise to you."

"Well," I answered, "all things considered, they have been a pleasant surprise; I may say a very pleasant surprise. And now let us go and have some dinner at the club. I feel tired and thirsty."

Next morning the letter that I had posted from London to the chairman of my committee was, at my request, returned to me unopened.

CHAPTER X

JANE MEETS DR. MERCHISON

Nobody disputed my inheritance, for, so far as I could learn, Mrs. Strong had no relatives. Nor indeed could it have been disputed, for I had never so much as hypnotised the deceased. When it was known how rich I had become I grew even more popular in Dunchester than I had been before, also my importance increased at headquarters to such an extent that on a change of Government I became, as I have said, Under-Secretary to the Home Office. Although I was a useful man hitherto I had always been refused any sort of office, because of the extreme views which I professed—on platforms in the constituencies—or so those in authority alleged. Now, however, these views were put down to amiable eccentricity; moreover, I was careful not to obtrude them. Responsibility sobers, and as we age and succeed we become more moderate, for most of us have a method in our madness.

In brief, I determined to give up political knight-errantry and to stick to sober business. Very carefully and in the most conservative spirit I took stock of the situation. I was still a couple of years on the right side of fifty, young looking for my age (an advantage), a desirable parti (a great advantage, although I had no intention of re-marrying), and in full health and vigour. Further, I possessed a large fortune all in cash or in liquid assets, and I resolved that it should not diminish. I had experienced enough of ups and downs; I was sick of vicissitudes, of fears and uncertainties for the future. I said to my soul: "Thou hast enough laid up for many days; eat, drink and be merry," and I proceeded to invest my modest competence in such a fashion that it brought in a steady four per cent. No South African mines or other soul-agonising speculations for me; sweet security was what I craved, and I got it. I could live with great comfort, even with modest splendour, upon about half my income, and the rest of it I purposed to lay out for my future benefit. I had observed that brewers, merchants and other magnates with cash to spare are in due course elevated to the peerage. Now I wished to be elevated to the peerage, and to spend an honoured and honourable old age as Lord Dunchester. So when there was any shortage of the party funds, and such a shortage soon occurred on the occasion of an election, I posed as the friend round the corner.

Moreover, I had another aim. My daughter Jane had now grown into a lovely, captivating and high-spirited young woman. To my fancy, indeed, I never saw her equal in appearance, for the large dark eyes shining in a fair and spirituelle face, encircled by masses of rippling chestnut hair, gave a bizarre and unusual distinction to her beauty, which was enhanced by a tall and graceful figure. She was witty also and self-willed, qualities which she inherited from her American mother, moreover she adored me and believed in me. I, who since my wife's death had loved nothing else, loved this pure and noble-minded girl as only a father can love, for my adoration had nothing selfish in it, whereas that of the truest lover, although he may not know it, is in its beginnings always selfish. He has something to gain, he seeks his own happiness, the father seeks only the happiness of his child.

On the whole, I think that the worship of this daughter of mine is a redeeming point in my character, for which otherwise, sitting in judgment on it as I do to-day, I have no respect. Jane understood that worship, and was grateful to me for it. Her fine unsullied instinct taught her that whatever else about me might be unsound or tarnished, this at least rang true and was beyond suspicion. She may have seen my open faults and divined my secret weaknesses, but for the sake of the love I bore her she overlooked them all, indeed she refused to acknowledge them, to the extent that my worst political extravagances became to her articles of faith. What I upheld was right; what I denounced was wrong; on other points her mind was open and intelligent, but on these it was a shut and bolted door. "My father says so," was her last argument.

My position being such that I could ensure her a splendid future, I was naturally anxious that she should make a brilliant marriage, since with monstrous injustice destiny has decreed that a woman's road to success must run past the altar. But as yet I could find no man whom I considered suitable or worthy. One or two I knew, but they were not peers, and I wished her to marry a peer or a rising politician who would earn or inherit a peerage.

And so, good easy man, I looked around me, and said that full surely my greatness was a-ripening. Who thinks of winter and its frosts in the glow of such a summer as I enjoyed?

For a while everything went well. I took a house in Green Street, and entertained there during the sitting of Parliament. The beauty of the hostess, my daughter Jane, together with my own position and wealth, of which she was the heiress, were sufficient to find us friends, or at any rate associates, among the noblest and most distinguished in the land, and for several seasons my dinner parties were some of the most talked about in London. To be asked to one of them was considered a compliment, even by men who are asked almost everywhere.

With such advantages of person, intelligence and surroundings at her command, Jane did not lack for opportunities of settling herself in life. To my knowledge she had three offers in one season, the last of them from perhaps the best and most satisfactory parti in England. But to my great and ever-increasing dismay, one after another she refused them all. The first two disappointments I bore, but on the third occasion I remonstrated. She listened quite quietly, then said:

"I am very sorry to vex you, father dear, but to marry a man whom I do not care about is just the one thing I can't do, even for your sake."

"But surely, Jane," I urged, "a father should have some voice in such a matter."

"I think he has a right to say whom his daughter shall not marry, perhaps, but not whom she shall marry."

"Then, at least," I said, catching at this straw, "will you promise that you won't become engaged to any one without my consent?"

Jane hesitated a little, and then answered: "What is the use of talking of such a thing, father, as I have never seen anybody to whom I wish to become engaged? But, if you like, I will promise you that if I should chance to see any one and you don't approve of him, I will not become engaged to him for three years, by the end of which time he would probably cease to wish to become engaged to me. But," she added with a laugh, "I am almost certain he wouldn't be a duke or a lord, or anything of that sort, for, provided a man is a gentleman, I don't care twopence about his having a title."

"Jane, don't talk so foolishly," I answered.

"Well, father," she said astonished, "if those are my opinions at least I got them from you, for I was always brought up upon strictly democratic principles. How often have I heard you declare in your lectures down at Dunchester that men of our race are all equal—except the working-man, who is better than the others—and that but for social prejudice the 'son of toil' is worthy of the hand of any titled lady in the kingdom?"

"I haven't delivered that lecture for years," I answered angrily.

"No, father, not since—let me see, not since old Mrs. Strong left you all her money, and you were made an Under-Secretary of State, and lords and ladies began to call on us. Now, I shouldn't have said that, because it makes you angry, but it is true, though, isn't it?" and she was gone.

That August when the House rose we went down to a place that I owned on the outskirts of Dunchester. It was a charming old house, situated in the midst of a considerable estate that is famous for its shooting. This property had come to me as part of Mrs. Strong's bequest, or, rather, she held a heavy mortgage on it, and when it was put up for sale I bought it in. As Jane had taken a fancy to the house, which was large and roomy, with beautiful gardens, I let my old home in the city, and when we were not in town we came to live at Ashfields.

On the borders of the Ashfields estate—indeed, part of the land upon which it was built belongs to it—lies a poor suburb of Dunchester occupied by workmen and their families. In these people Jane took great interest; indeed, she plagued me till at very large expense I built a number of model cottages for them, with electricity, gas and water laid on, and bicycle-houses attached. In fact, this proved a futile proceeding, for the only result was that the former occupants of the dwellings were squeezed out, while persons of a better class, such as clerks, took possession of the model tenements at a totally inadequate rent.

It was in visiting some of the tenants of these cottages that in an evil hour Jane first met Dr. Merchison, a young man of about thirty, who held some parish appointment which placed the sick of this district under his charge. Ernest Merchison was a raw-boned, muscular and rather formidable-looking person, of Scotch descent, with strongly-marked features, deep-set eyes, and very long arms. A man of few words, when he did speak his language was direct to the verge of brusqueness, but his record as a medical man was good and even distinguished, and already he had won the reputation of being the best surgeon in Dunchester. This was the individual who was selected by my daughter Jane to receive the affections which she had refused to some of the most polished and admired men in England, and, as I believe, largely for the reason that, instead of bowing and sighing about after her, he treated her with a rudeness which was almost brutal.

In one of these new model houses lived some people of the name of Smith. Mr. Smith was a compositor, and Mrs. Smith, nee Samuels, was none other than that very little girl whom, together with her brother, who died, I had once treated for erysipelas resulting from vaccination. In a way I felt grateful to her, for that case was the beginning of my real success in life, and for this reason, out of several applicants, the new model house was let to her husband as soon as it was ready for occupation.

Could I have foreseen the results which were to flow from an act of kindness, and that as this family had indirectly been the cause of my triumph so they were in turn to be the cause of my ruin, I would have destroyed the whole street with dynamite before I allowed them to set foot in it. However, they came, bringing with them two children, a little girl of four, to whom Jane took a great fancy, and a baby of eighteen months.

In due course these children caught the whooping-cough, and Jane visited them, taking with her some delicacies as a present. While she was there Dr. Merchison arrived in his capacity of parish doctor, and, beyond a curt bow taking no notice of Jane, began his examination, for this was his first visit to the family. Presently his eye fell upon a box of sweets.

"What's that?" he asked sharply.

"It's a present that Miss Therne here has brought for Tottie," answered the mother.

"Then Tottie mustn't eat them till she is well. Sugar is bad for whooping-cough, though, of course, a young lady couldn't be expected to know that," he added in a voice of gruff apology, then went on quickly, glancing at the little girl's arm, "No marks, I see. Conscientious Objector? Or only lazy?"

Then Mrs. Smith fired up and poured out her own sad history and that of her poor little brother who died, baring her scarred arm in proof of it.

"And so," she finished, "though I do not remember much about it myself, I do remember my mother's dying words, which were 'to mind what the doctor had told her, and never to have any child of mine vaccinated, no, not if they crawled on their knees to ask it of me.'"

"The doctor!" said Merchison with scorn, "you mean the idiot, my good woman, or more likely the political agitator who would sell his soul for a billet."

Then Jane rose in wrath.

"I beg your pardon for interrupting you, sir," she said, "but the gentleman you speak of as an idiot or a political agitator is Dr. Therne, my father, the member of Parliament for this city."

Dr. Merchison stared at her for a long while, and indeed when she was angry Jane was beautiful enough to make any one stare, then he said simply, "Oh, indeed. I don't meddle with politics, so I didn't know."

This was too much for Jane, who, afraid to trust herself to further speech, walked straight out of the cottage. She had passed down the model garden and arrived at the model gate when she heard a quick powerful step behind her, and turned round to find herself face to face with Dr. Merchison.

"I have followed you to apologise, Miss Therne," he said; "of course I had no idea who you were and did not wish to hurt your feelings, but I happen to have strong feelings about vaccination and spoke more roughly than I ought to have done."

"Other people, sir, may also have strong opinions about vaccination," answered Jane.

"I know," he said, "and I know, too, what the end of it all will be, as you will also, Miss Therne, if you live long enough. It is useless arguing, the lists are closed and we must wait until the thing is put to the proof of battle. When it is, one thing is sure, there will be plenty of dead," he added with a grim smile. Then taking off his hat and muttering, "Again I apologise," he returned into the cottage.

It seems that for a while Jane was very angry. Then she remembered that, after all, Dr. Merchison had apologised, and that he had made his offensive remarks in the ignorance and prejudice which afflicted the entire medical profession and were more worthy of pity than of anger. Further, she remembered that in her indignation she had forgotten to acknowledge or accept his apology, and, lastly, she asked him to a garden-party.

It is scarcely necessary for me to dwell upon the subsequent developments of this unhappy business—if I am right in calling it unhappy. The piteous little drama is played, both the actors are dead, and the issue of the piece is unknown and, for the present, unknowable. Bitterly opposed as I was to the suit of Merchison, justice compels me to say that, under the cloak of a rough unpromising manner, he hid a just and generous heart. Had that man lived he might have become great, although he would never have become popular. As least something in his nature attracted my daughter Jane, for she, who up to that time had not been moved by any man, became deeply attached to him.

In the end he proposed to her, how, when or where I cannot say, for I never inquired. One morning, I remember it was that of Christmas day, they came into my library, the pair of them, and informed me how matters stood. Merchison went straight to the point and put the case before me very briefly, but in a manly and outspoken fashion. He said that he quite understood the difficulties of his position, inasmuch as he believed that Jane was, or would be, very rich, whereas he had nothing beyond his profession, in which, however, he was doing well. He ended by asking my consent to the engagement subject to any reasonable conditions that I might choose to lay down.

To me the shock was great, for, occupied as I was with my own affairs and ambitions, I had been blind to what was passing before my face. I had hoped to see my daughter a peeress, and now I found her the affianced bride of a parish sawbones. The very foundation of my house of hopes was sapped; at a blow all my schemes for the swift aggrandisement of my family were laid low. It was too much for me. Instead of accepting the inevitable, and being glad to accept it because my child's happiness was involved, I rebelled and kicked against the pricks.

By nature I am not a violent man, but on that occasion I lost my temper and became violent. I refused my consent; I threatened to cut my daughter off with nothing, but at this argument she and her lover smiled. Then I took another ground, for, remembering her promise that she would consent to be separated for three years from any suitor of whom I did not approve, I claimed its fulfilment.

Somewhat to my surprise, after a hurried private consultation, Jane and her lover accepted these conditions, telling me frankly that they would wait for three years, but that after these had gone by they would consider themselves at liberty to marry, with my consent if possible, but, if necessary, without it. Then in my presence they kissed and parted, nor until the last did either of them attempt to break the letter of their bond. Once indeed they met before that dreadful hour, but then it was the workings of fate that brought them together and not their own design.

CHAPTER XI

THE COMING OF THE RED-HEADED MAN

Half of the three years of probation had gone by and once more we found ourselves at Dunchester in August. Under circumstances still too recent to need explanation, the Government of which I was a member had decided to appeal to the country, the General Election being fixed for the end of September, after the termination of harvest. Dunchester was considered to be a safe Radical seat, and, as a matter of parliamentary tactics, the poll for this city, together with that of eight or ten other boroughs, was fixed for the earliest possible day, in the hope that the results might encourage more doubtful places to give their support. Constituencies are very like sheep, and if the leaders jump through a certain gap in the political hedge the flock, or a large proportion of it, will generally follow. All of us like to be on the winning side.

Few people who are old enough to remember it will ever forget the August of two years ago, if only because of the phenomenal heat. Up to that month the year had been very cold, so cold that even during July there were some evenings when a fire was welcome, while on several days I saw people driving about the roads wrapped up in heavy ulsters. But with the first day of August all this changed, and suddenly the climate became torrid, the nights especially being extraordinarily hot. From every quarter of the country came complaints of the great heat, while each issue of the newspapers contained lists of those who had fallen victims to it.

One evening, feeling oppressed in the tree-enclosed park of Ashfields, I strolled out of it into the suburb of which I have spoken. Almost opposite the private garden of the park stands a board school, and in front of this board school I had laid out an acre of land presented by myself, as a playground and open space for the use of the public. In the centre of this garden was a fountain that fell into a marble basin, and around the fountain, but at some distance from it, stood iron seats. To these I made my way and sat down on one of them, which was empty, in order to enjoy the cool sound of the splashing water, about which a large number of children were playing.

Presently, as I sat thus, I lifted my eyes and saw the figure of a man approaching towards the other side of the fountain. He was quite fifty yards away from me, so that his features were invisible, but there was something about his general aspect which attracted my attention at once. To begin with, he looked small and lonely, all by himself out there on the wide expanse of gravel; moreover, the last rays of the setting sun, striking full upon him, gave him a fiery and unnatural appearance against the dense background of shadows beyond. It is a strange and dreadful coincidence, but by some extraordinary action of the mind, so subtle that I cannot trace the link, the apparition of this man out of the gloom into the fierce light of the sunset reminded me of a picture that I had once seen representing the approach to the Norwegian harbour of the ship which brought the plague to the shores of Scandanavia. In the picture that ship also was clothed with the fires of sunset, while behind it lay the blackness of approaching night. Like this wanderer that ship also came forward, slowly indeed, but without pause, as though alive with a purpose of its own, and I remember that awaiting it upon the quay were a number of merry children.

Shaking myself free from this ridiculous but unpleasant thought, I continued to observe the man idly. Clearly he was one of the great army of tramps, for his coat was wide and ragged and his hat half innocent of rim, although there was something about his figure which suggested to me that he had seen better days. I could even imagine that under certain circumstances I might have come to look very much like this poor man, now doubtless turned into a mere animal by drink. He drew on with a long slow step, his head stretched forward, his eyes fixed upon the water, as he walked now and again lifting a long thin hand and scraping impatiently at his face and head.

"That poor fellow has got a touch of prickly heat and is thirsty," I thought, nor was I mistaken, for, on arriving at the edge of the fountain, the tramp knelt down and drank copiously, making a moaning sound as he gulped the water, which was very peculiar and unpleasant to hear. When he had satisfied his thirst, he sat himself upon the marble edge of the basin and suddenly plunged his legs, boots and all, into the water. Its touch seemed to please him, for with a single swift movement he slipped in altogether, sitting himself down on the bottom of the basin in such fashion that only his face and fiery red beard, from which the hat had fallen, remained above the surface, whereon they seemed to float like some monstrous and unnatural growth.

This unusual proceeding on the part of the tramping stranger at once excited the most intense interest in the mind of every child on the playground, with the result that in another minute forty or fifty of them had gathered round the fountain, laughing and jeering at its occupant. Again the sight brought to my mind a strained and disagreeable simile, for I bethought me of the dreadful tale of Elisha and of the fate which overtook the children who mocked him. Decidedly the heat had upset my nerves that night, nor were they soothed when suddenly from the red head floating upon the water came a flute-like and educated voice, saying—

"Cease deriding the unfortunate, children, or I will come out of this marble bath and tickle you."

Thereat they laughed all the more, and began to pelt the bather with little stones and bits of stick.

At first I thought of interfering, but as it occurred to me that the man would probably be violent or abusive if I spoke to him, and as, above all things, I disliked scenes, I made up my mind to fetch a policeman, whom I knew I should find round the corner about a hundred yards away. I walked to the corner, but did not find the policeman, whereon I started across the square to look for him at another point. My road led me past the fountain, and, as I approached it, I saw that the water-loving wanderer had been as good as his word. He had emerged from the fountain, and, rushing to and fro raining moisture from his wide coat, despite their shrieks half of fear and half of laughter, he grabbed child after child and, drawing it to him, tickled and kissed it, laughing dementedly all the while, in a fashion which showed me that he was suffering from some form of mania.

As soon as he saw me the man dropped the last child he had caught—it was little Tottie Smith—and began to stride away towards the city at the same slow, regular, purposeful gait with which I had seen him approach the fountain. As he passed he turned and made a grimace at me, and then I saw his dreadful face. No wonder it had looked red at a distance, for the erythema almost covered it, except where, on the forehead and cheeks, appeared purple spots and patches.

Of what did it remind me?

Great Heaven! I remembered. It reminded me of the face of that girl I had seen lying in the plaza of San Jose, in Mexico, over whom the old woman was pouring water from the fountain, much such a fountain as that before me, for half unconsciously, when planning this place, I had reproduced its beautiful design. It all came back to me with a shock, the horrible scene of which I had scarcely thought for years, so vividly indeed that I seemed to hear the old hag's voice crying in cracked accents, "Si, senor, viruela, viruela!"

I ought to have sent to warn the police and the health officers of the city, for I was sure that the man was suffering from what is commonly called confluent smallpox. But I did not. From the beginning there has been something about this terrible disease which physically and morally has exercised so great an influence over my destiny, that seemed to paralyse my mental powers. In my day I was a doctor fearless of any other contagion, typhus, scarletina, diphtheria, yellow fever, none of them had terrors for me. And yet I was afraid to attend a case of smallpox. From the same cause, in my public speeches I made light of it, talking of it with contempt as a sickness of small account, much as a housemaid talks in the servants' hall of the ghost which is supposed to haunt the back stairs.

And now, coming as it were from that merry and populous chamber of life and health, once again I met the Spectre I derided, a red-headed, red-visaged Thing that chose me out to stop and grin at. Somehow I was not minded to return and announce the fact.

"Why," they would say, "you were the one who did not believe in ghosts. It was you who preached of vile superstitions, and yet merely at the sight of a shadow you rush in with trembling hands and bristling hair to bid us lay it with bell, book, and candle. Where is your faith, O prophet?"

It was nonsense; the heat and all my incessant political work had tried me and I was mistaken. That tramp was a drunken, or perhaps a crazy creature, afflicted with some skin disease such as are common among his class. Why did I allow the incident to trouble me?

I went home and washed out my mouth, and sprinkled my clothes with a strong solution of permanganate of potash, for, although my own folly was evident, it is always as well to be careful, especially in hot weather. Still I could not help wondering what might happen if by any chance smallpox were to get a hold of a population like that of Dunchester, or indeed of a hundred other places in England.

Since the passing of the famous Conscience Clause many years before, as was anticipated would be the case, and as the anti-vaccinators intended should be the case, vaccination had become a dead letter amongst at least seventy-five per cent. of the people.[*] Our various societies and agents were not content to let things take their course and to allow parents to vaccinate their children, or to leave them unvaccinated as they might think fit. On the contrary, we had instituted a house-to-house canvass, and our visitors took with them forms of conscientious objection, to be filled in by parents or guardians, and legally witnessed.

[*] *Since the above was written the author has read in the press that in Yorkshire a single bench of magistrates out of the hundreds in England has already granted orders on the ground of "conscientious objection," under which some 2000 children are exempted from the scope of the Vaccination Acts. So far as he has seen this statement has not been contradicted. At Ipswich also about 700 applications, affecting many children, have been filed. To deal with these the Bench is holding special sessions, sitting at seven o'clock in the evening.*

At first the magistrates refused to accept these forms, but after a while, when they found how impossible it was to dive into a man's conscience and to decide what was or what was not "conscientious objection," they received them as sufficient evidence, provided only that they were sworn before some one entitled to administer oaths. Many of the objectors did not even take the trouble to do as much as this, for within five years of the passing of the Act, in practice the vaccination laws ceased to exist. The burden of prosecution rested with Boards of Guardians, popularly elected bodies, and what board was likely to go to the trouble of working up a case and to the expense of bringing it before the court, when, to produce a complete defence, the defendant need only declare that he had a conscientious objection to the law under which the information was laid against him? Many idle or obstinate or prejudiced people would develop conscientious objections to anything which gives trouble or that they happen to dislike. For instance, if the same principle were applied to education, I believe that within a very few years not twenty-five per cent. of the children belonging to the classes that are educated out of the rates would ever pass the School Board standards.

Thus it came about that the harvest was ripe, and over ripe, awaiting only the appointed sickle of disease. Once or twice already that sickle had been put in, but always before the reaping began it was stayed by the application of the terrible rule of isolation known as the improved Leicester system.

Among some of the natives of Africa when smallpox breaks out in a kraal, that kraal is surrounded by guards and its inhabitants are left to recover or perish, to starve or to feed themselves as chance and circumstance may dictate. During the absence of the smallpox laws the same plan, more mercifully applied, prevailed in England, and thus the evil hour was postponed. But it was only postponed, for like a cumulative tax it was heaping up against the country, and at last the hour had come for payment to an authority whose books must be balanced without remittance or reduction. What is due to nature that nature takes in her own way and season, neither less nor more, unless indeed the skill and providence of man can find means to force her to write off the debt.

Five days after my encounter with the red-headed vagrant, the following paragraph appeared in one of the local papers: "Pocklingham. In the casual ward of the Union house for this district a tramp, name unknown, died last night. He had been admitted on the previous evening, but, for some unexplained reason, it was not noticed until the next morning that he suffered from illness, and, therefore, he was allowed to mix with the other inmates in the general ward. Drs. Butt and Clarkson, who were called in to attend, state that the cause of death was the worst form of smallpox. The body will be buried in quicklime, but some alarm is felt in the district owing to the deceased, who, it is said, arrived here from Dunchester, where he had been frequenting various tramps' lodgings, having mixed with a number of other vagrants, who left the house before the character of his sickness was discovered, and who cannot now be traced. The unfortunate man was about forty years of age, of medium height, and red-haired."

The same paper had an editorial note upon this piece of news, at the end of which it remarked, as became a party and an anti-vaccination organ: "The terror of this 'filth disease,' which in our fathers' time amounted almost to insanity, no longer afflicts us, who know both that its effects were exaggerated and how to deal with it by isolation without recourse to the so-called vaccine remedies, which are now rejected by a large proportion of the population of these islands. Still, as we have ascertained by inquiry that this unfortunate man did undoubtedly spend several days and nights wandering about our city when in an infectious condition, it will be as well that the authorities should be on the alert. We do not want that hoary veteran—the smallpox scare—to rear its head again in Dunchester, least of all just now, when, in view of the imminent election, the accustomed use would be made of it by our prejudiced and unscrupulous political opponents."

"No," I said to myself as I put the paper down, "certainly we do not want a smallpox scare just now, and still less do we want the smallpox." Then I thought of that unfortunate red-headed wretch, crazy with the torment of his disease, and of his hideous laughter, as he hunted and caught the children who made a mock of him—the poor children, scarcely one of whom was vaccinated.

A week later I opened my political campaign with a large public meeting in the Agricultural Hall. Almost up to the nomination day no candidate was forthcoming on the other side, and I thought that, for the fourth time, I should be returned unopposed. Of a sudden, however, a name was announced, and it proved to be none other than that of my rival of many years ago—Sir Thomas Colford—now like myself growing grey-headed, but still vigorous in mind and body, and as much respected as ever by the wealthier and more educated classes of our community. His appearance in the field put a new complexion on matters; it meant, indeed, that instead of the easy and comfortable walk over which I had anticipated, I must fight hard for my political existence.

In the course of my speech, which was very well received, for I was still popular in the town even among the more moderate of my opponents, I dwelt upon Sir Thomas Colford's address to the electorate which had just come into my hands. In this address I was astonished to see a paragraph advocating, though in a somewhat guarded fashion, the re-enactment of the old laws of compulsory vaccination. In a draft which had reached me two days before through some underground channel, this paragraph had not appeared, thus showing that it had been added by an afterthought and quite suddenly. However, there it was, and I made great play with it.

What, I asked the electors of Dunchester, could they think of a man who in these modern and enlightened days sought to reimpose upon a free people the barbarous infamies of the Vaccination Acts? Long ago we had fought that fight, and long ago we had relegated them to limbo, where, with such things as instruments of torment, papal bulls and writs of attainder, they remained to excite the wonder and the horror of our own and future generations.

Well would it have been for me if I had stopped here, but, led away by the subject and by the loud cheers that my treatment of it, purposely flamboyant, never failed to evoke, forgetful too for the moment of the Red-headed Man, I passed on to deductions. Our opponents had prophesied, I said, that within ten years of the passing of the famous Conscience Clause smallpox would be rampant. Now what were the facts? Although almost twice that time had gone by, here in Dunchester we had suffered far less from smallpox than during the compulsory period, for at no one time during all these eighteen or twenty years had three cases been under simultaneous treatment within the confines of the city.

"Well, there are five now," called out a voice from the back of the hall.

I drew myself up and made ready to wither this untruthful brawler with my best election scorn, when, of a sudden, I remembered the Red-headed Man, and passed on to the consideration of foreign affairs.

From that moment all life went out of my speech, and, as it seemed to me, the enthusiasm of the meeting died away. As soon as it was over I made inquiries, to find that the truth had been hidden from me—there were five, if not seven cases of smallpox in different parts of the city, and the worst feature of the facts was that three of the patients were children attending different schools. One of these children, it was ascertained, had been among those who were playing round the fountain about a fortnight since, although he was not one whom the red-haired tramp had touched, but the other two had not been near the fountain. The presumption was, therefore, that they had contracted the disease through some other source of infection, perhaps at the lodging-house where the man had spent the night after bathing in the water. Also it seemed that, drawn thither by the heat, in all two or three hundred children had visited the fountain square on this particular evening, and that many of them had drunk water out of the basin.

Never do I remember feeling more frightened than when these facts came to my knowledge, for, added to the possible terrors of the position, was my constitutional fear of the disease which I have already described. On my way homewards I met a friend who told me that one of the children was dead, the malady, which was of an awful type, having done its work very swiftly.

Like a first flake from a snow-cloud, like a first leaf falling in autumn from among the myriads on some great tree, so did this little life sink from our number into the silence of the grave. Ah! how many were to follow? There is a record, I believe, but I cannot give it. In Dunchester alone, with its population of about 50,000, I know that we had over 5000 deaths, and Dunchester was a focus from which the pestilence spread through the kingdom, destroying and destroying and destroying with a fury that has not been equalled since the days of the Black Death.

But all this was still to come, for the plague did not get a grip at once. An iron system of isolation was put in force, and every possible means was adopted by the town authorities, who, for the most part, were anti-vaccinationists, to suppress the facts, a task in which they were assisted by the officials of the Local Government Board, who had their instructions on the point. As might have been expected, the party in power did not wish the political position to be complicated by an outcry for the passing of a new smallpox law, so few returns were published, and as little information as possible was given to the papers.

For a while there was a lull; the subject of smallpox was taboo, and nobody heard much about it beyond vague and indefinite rumours. Indeed, most of us were busy with the question of the hour—the eternal question of beer, its purity and the method of its sale. For my part, I made few inquiries; like the ostrich of fable I hid my head in the sands of political excitement, hoping that the arrows of pestilence would pass us by.

And yet, although I breathed no word of my fears to a living soul, in my heart I was terribly afraid.

CHAPTER XII

THE SHADOW OF PESTILENCE

Very soon it became evident that the fight in Dunchester would be severe, for the electorate, which for so many years had been my patient servant, showed signs of rebelling against me and the principles I preached. Whether the voters were moved by a desire for change, whether they honestly disagreed with me, or whether a secret fear of the smallpox was the cause of it, I do not know, but it is certain that a large proportion of them began to look upon me and my views with distrust.

At any other time this would not have caused me great distress; indeed defeat itself would have had consolations, but now, when I appeared to be on the verge of real political distinction, the mere thought of failure struck me with dismay. To avoid it, I worked as I had not worked for years. Meetings were held nightly, leaflets were distributed by the ton, and every house in the city was industriously visited by my canvassers, who were divided into bands and officers like a regiment.

The head of one of these bands was my daughter Jane, and never did a candidate have a more able or enthusiastic lieutenant. She was gifted with the true political instinct, which taught her what to say and what to leave unsaid, when to press a point home and when to abandon it for another; moreover, her personal charm and popularity fought for her cause.

One evening, as she was coming home very tired after a long day's work in the slums of the city, Jane arrived at the model cottages outside my park gates. Having half an hour to spare, she determined to visit a few of their occupants. Her second call was on the Smith family.

"I am glad to see you now as always, miss," said Mrs. Smith, "but we are in trouble here."

"What, is little Tottie ill again?" Jane asked.

"No, miss, it isn't Tottie this time, it's the baby. She's got convulsions, or something like it, and I've sent for Dr. Merchison. Would you like to see her? She's lying in the front room."

Jane hesitated. She was tired and wanted to get home with her canvass cards. But the woman looked tired too and in need of sympathy; possibly also, for nature is nature, Jane hoped that if she lingered there a little, without in any way violating her promise, she might chance to catch a brief glimpse of the man she loved.

"Yes, I will come in for a minute," she answered and followed Mrs. Smith into the room.

On a cheap cane couch in the corner, at the foot of which the child, Tottie, was playing with a doll, lay the baby, an infant of nearly three. The convulsive fit had passed away and she was sitting up supported by a pillow, the fair hair hanging about her flushed face, and beating the blanket with her little fevered hands.

"Take me, mummy, take me, I thirsty," she moaned.

"There, that's how she goes on all day and it fairly breaks my heart to see her," said the mother, wiping away a tear with her apron. "If you'll be so kind as to mind her a minute, miss, I'll go and make a little lemonade. I've got a couple of oranges left, and she seems to like them best of anything."

Jane's heart was stirred, and, leaning down, she took the child in her arms. "Go and get the drink," she said, "I will look after her till you come," and she began to walk up and down the room rocking the little sufferer to and fro.

Presently she looked up to see Dr. Merchison standing in the doorway.

"Jane, you here!" he said.

"Yes, Ernest."

He stepped towards her, and, before she could turn away or remonstrate, bent down and kissed her on the lips.

"You shouldn't do that, dear," she said, "it's out of the bargain."

"Perhaps I shouldn't," he answered, "but I couldn't help it. I said that I would keep clear of you, and if I have met you by accident it is not my fault. Come, let me have a look at that child."

Taking the little girl upon his knee, he began to examine her, feeling her pulse and looking at her tongue. For a while he seemed puzzled, then Jane saw him take a little magnifying glass from his pocket and by the help of it search the skin of the patient's forehead, especially just at the roots of the hair. After this he looked at the neck and wrists, then set the child down on the couch, waving Jane back when she advanced to take it, and asked the mother, who had just entered the room with the lemonade, two or three short, quick questions.

Next he turned to Jane and said—

"I don't want to frighten you, but you will be as well out of this. It's lucky for you," he added with a little smile, "that when you were born it wasn't the fashion for doctors to be anti-vaccinationists, for, unless I am much mistaken, that child has got smallpox."

"Smallpox!" said Jane, then added aggressively, "Well, now we shall see whose theory is right, for, as you saw, I was nursing her, and I have never been vaccinated in my life. My father would not allow it, and I have been told that it won him his first election."

Ernest Merchison heard, and for a moment his face became like that of a man in a fit.

"The wicked—" he began, and stopped himself by biting his lips till the blood came. Recovering his calm with an effort, he turned to Jane and said in a hoarse voice:—

"There is still a chance; it may be in time; yes, I am almost sure that I can save you." Then he plunged his hand into his breast pocket and drew out a little case of instruments. "Be so good as to bare your left arm," he said; "fortunately, I have the stuff with me."

"What for?" she asked.

"To be vaccinated."

"Are you mad, Ernest?" she said. "You know who I am and how I have been brought up; how, then, can you suppose that I would allow you to put that poison into my veins?"

"Look here, Jane, there isn't much time for argument, but just listen to me for one minute. You know I am a pretty good doctor, don't you? for I have that reputation, haven't I? and I am sure that you believe in me. Well, now, just on this one point and for this one occasion I am going to ask you to give up your own opinion and to suppose that in this matter I am right and your father is wrong. I will go farther, and say that if any harm comes to you from this vaccination beyond the inconvenience of a swollen arm, you may consider all that has been between us as nothing and never speak to me again."

"That's not the point," she answered. "If you vaccinated me and my arm fell off in consequence I shouldn't care for you a bit the less, because I should know that you were the victim of a foolish superstition, and believed what you were doing to be right. No, Ernest, it is of no use; I can assure you that I know a great deal more about this subject than you do. I have read all the papers and statistics and heard the cleverest men in England lecture upon it, and nothing, nothing, nothing will ever induce me to submit to that filthy, that revolting operation."

He heard and groaned, then he tried another argument.

"Listen," he said: "you have been good enough to tell me—several times—well, that you loved me, and, forgive me for alluding to it, but I think that once you were so foolish as to say that you cared for me so much that you would give your very existence if it could make me happy. Now, I ask you for nothing half so great as that; I ask you to submit to a trifling inconvenience, and, so far as you are personally concerned, to waive a small prejudice for my sake, or, perhaps I had better say, to give in to my folly. Can't you do as much as that for me, Jane?"

"Ernest," she answered hoarsely, "if you asked anything else of me in the world I would do it—yes, anything you can think of—but this I can't do and won't do."

"In God's name, why not?" he cried.

"Because to do it would be to declare my father a quack and a liar, and to show that I, his daughter, from whom if from anybody he has a right to expect faith and support, have no belief in him and the doctrine that he has taught for twenty years. That is the truth, and it is cruel of you to make me say it."

Ernest Merchison ground his teeth, understanding that in face of this woman's blind fidelity all argument and appeal were helpless. Then in his love and despair he formed a desperate resolve. Yes, he was very strong, and he thought that he could do it.

Catching her suddenly round the waist he thrust her into a cottage armchair which stood by, and, despite her struggles, began to cut at the sleeve of her dress with the lancet in his hand. But soon he realised that the task was hopeless.

"Ernest Merchison," she said, as she escaped from him with blazing eyes and catching breath, "you have done what I will never forgive. Go your own way in life and I will go mine."

"—To death, Jane."

Then she walked out of the house and through the garden gate. When she had gone ten or fifteen yards she looked back to see her lover standing by the gate, his face buried in his hands, and his strong frame shaking with sobs. For a moment Jane relented; it was terrible to see this reserved and self-reliant man thus weeping openly, and she knew that the passion must be mighty which would bring him to this pass. In her heart, indeed, she had never loved him better than at this moment; she loved him even for his brutal attempt to vaccinate her by force, because she understood what instigated the brutality. But then she remembered the insult—she to be seized like a naughty child who will not take its dose, and in the presence of another woman. And, so remembering, she hardened her heart and passed out of his sight towards the gateways of the grave.

At that time Jane said nothing of her adventure to me, though afterwards I learned every detail of it from her and Mrs. Smith. She did not even tell me that she had visited the Smiths' cottage until one morning, about eight days afterwards, when some blundering servant informed us at breakfast that the baby Smith was dead of the smallpox in the hospital, and that the other child was dangerously ill. I was shocked beyond measure, for this brought the thing home, the people lived almost at my gates. Now I remembered that I had seen the red-headed tramp catch the child Tottie in his arms. Doubtless she introduced the infection, though, strangely enough, her little sister developed the disease before her.

"Jane," I said when the servant had left, "did you hear about the Smith baby?"

"Yes, father," she answered languidly, "I knew that it had smallpox a week ago."

"Then why did you not tell me, and how did you know?"

"I didn't tell you, dear, because the mere mention of smallpox always upsets you so much, especially just now with all this election worry going on; and I knew it because I was at the Smiths' cottage and nursing the baby when the doctor came in and said it was smallpox."

"You were nursing the baby!" I almost screamed as I sprang from my seat. "Great heavens, girl; why, you will infect the whole place."

"That was what Ernest—Dr. Merchison—seemed to think. He wanted to vaccinate me."

"Oh, and did you let him?"

"How can you ask me such a question, father, remembering what you have always taught me? I said—" and with omissions she told me the gist of what had passed between them.

"I didn't mean that," I answered when she had done. "I thought that perhaps under the influence of shock—Well, as usual, you showed your wisdom, for how can one poison kill another poison?" and, unable to bear it any longer, making some excuse, I rose and left the room.

Her wisdom! Great heavens, her wisdom! Why did not that fool, Merchison, insist? He should have authority over her if any man had. And now it was too late—now no vaccination on earth could save her, unless by chance she had escaped infection, which was scarcely to be hoped. Indeed, such a thing was hardly known as that an unvaccinated person coming into immediate contact with a smallpox patient after the eruption had appeared, should escape infection.

What did this mean? It meant that within a few days Jane, my only and darling child, the very hope and centre of my life, would be in the fangs of one of the most dreadful and dangerous diseases known to humanity. More, having never been vaccinated, that disease was sure to strike her with its full force, and the type of it which had appeared in the city was such that certainly not more than one-half of the unprotected persons attacked came alive out of the struggle.

This was bad enough, but there were other things behind. I had never been vaccinated since infancy, over fifty years ago, and was therefore practically unprotected with the enemy that all my lifetime I had dreaded, as I dreaded no other thing or imagination, actually standing at my door. I could not go away because of the election; I dared not show fear, because they would cry: "Look at the hangman when he sees the rope." Here, since compulsory vaccination had been abandoned, we fought smallpox by a system of isolation so rigorous that under its cruel provisions every one of whatever age, rank or sex in whom the disease declared itself was instantly removed to a hospital, while the inhabitants of the house whence the patient came were kept practically in prison, not being allowed to mix with their fellows. We had returned to the preventive measures of centuries ago, much as they were practised in the time of the Great Plague.

But how could I send my daughter to one of those dreadful pest-pits, there at the moment of struggle to be a standing advertisement of the utter failure and falsity of the system I had preached, backing my statements with the wager of her life? Moreover, to do so would be to doom myself to defeat at the poll, since under our byelaws, which were almost ferocious in their severity, I could no longer appear in public to prosecute my canvass, and, if my personal influence was withdrawn, then most certainly my adversary would win.

Oh, truly I who had sown bounteously was reaping bounteously. Truly the birds which I had sent out on their mission of evil had come home to roost upon my roof-tree.

CHAPTER XIII

HARVEST

Another five days went by—to me they were days of most unspeakable doubt and anguish. Each morning at breakfast I waited for the coming of Jane with an anxiety which was all the more dreadful because I forced myself to conceal it. There had been no further conversation between us about the matter that haunted both our minds, and so fearful was I lest she should divine my suspense that except in the most casual way I did not even dare to look at her as she entered the room.

On the fifth morning she was late for breakfast, not a common thing, for as a rule she rose early. I sent one of the parlour-maids to her room to ask if she was coming down, and stood awaiting the answer with much the same feeling as a criminal on his trial awaits the verdict of the jury. Presently the girl returned with the message that Miss Therne would be down in a few minutes, whereat I breathed again and swallowed a little food, which till then I had been unable to touch.

Soon she came, and I saw that she was rather pale and languid, owing to the heat, perhaps, but that otherwise she looked much as usual.

"You are late, dear," I said unconcernedly.

"Yes, father," she answered; "I woke up with a little headache and went to sleep again. It has gone now; I suppose that it is the heat."

As she spoke she kissed me, and I thought—but this may have been fancy—that her breath felt cold upon my cheek.

"I daresay," I said, and we sat down to table. By my plate lay a great pile of correspondence, which I opened while making pretence to eat, but all the time I was watching Jane over the top of those wearisome letters, most of them from beggars or constituents who "wanted to know." One, however, was anonymous, from a person who signed herself "Mother." It ran:—

"Sir,—After hearing your speeches some years ago, and being told that you were such a clever man, I became a Conscientious Objector, and would not let them vaccinate any more of my children. The three who were not vaccinated have all been taken to the hospital with the smallpox, and they tell me (for I am not allowed to see them) that one of them is dead; but the two who were vaccinated are quite well. Sir, I thought that you would like to know this, so that if you have made any mistake you may tell others. Sir, forgive me for troubling you, but it is a terrible thing to have one's child die of smallpox, and, as I acted on your advice, I take the liberty of writing the above."

Again I looked at Jane, and saw that although she was sipping her tea and had some bacon upon her plate she had eaten nothing at all. Like the catch of a song echoed through my brain that fearsome sentence: "It is a terrible thing to have one's child die of the smallpox." Terrible, indeed, for now I had little doubt but that Jane was infected, and if she should chance to die, then what should I be? I should be her murderer!

After breakfast I started upon my rounds of canvassing and speech-making. Oh, what a dreadful day was that, and how I loathed the work. How I cursed the hour in which I had taken up politics, and sold my honour to win a seat in Parliament and a little cheap notoriety among my fellow-men. If Stephen Strong had not tempted me Jane would have been vaccinated in due course, and therefore, good friend though he had been to me, and though his wealth was mine to-day, I cursed the memory of Stephen Strong. Everywhere I went that afternoon I heard ominous whispers. People did not talk openly; they shrugged their shoulders and nodded and hinted, and all their hints had to do with the smallpox.

"I say, Therne," said an old friend, the chairman of my committee, with a sudden outburst of candour, "what a dreadful thing it would be if after all we A.V.'s were mistaken. You know there are a good many cases of it about, for it's no use disguising the truth. But I haven't heard of any yet among the Calf-worshippers" (that was our cant term for those who believed in vaccination).

"Oh, let be!" I answered angrily, "it is too late to talk of mistakes, we've got to see this thing through."

"Yes, yes, Therne," he said with a dreary laugh, "unless it should happen to see us through."

I left him, and went home just in time to dress. There were some people to dinner, at which Jane appeared. Her lassitude had vanished, and, as was her manner when in good spirits, she was very humorous and amusing. Also I had never seen her look so beautiful, for her colour was high and her dark eyes shone like the diamond stars in her hair. But again I observed that she ate nothing, although she, who for the most part drank little but water, took several glasses of champagne and two tumblers of soda. Before I could get rid of my guests she had gone to bed. At length they went, and going to my study I began to smoke and think.

I was now sure that the bright flush upon her cheeks was due to what we doctors call pyrexia, the initial fever of smallpox, and that the pest which I had dreaded and fled from all my life was established in my home. The night was hot and I had drunk my fill of wine, but I sat and shook in the ague of my fear. Jane had the disease, but she was young and strong and might survive it. I should take it from her, and in that event assuredly must die, for the mind is master of the body and the thing we dread is the thing that kills us.

Probably, indeed, I had taken it already, and this very moment the seeds of sickness were at their wizard work within me. Well, even if it was so?—I gasped when the thought struck me—as Merchison had recognised in the case of Jane, by immediate vaccination the virus could be destroyed, or if not destroyed at least so much modified and weakened as to become almost harmless. Smallpox takes thirteen or fourteen days to develop; cowpox runs its course in eight. So even supposing that I had been infected for two days there was still time. Yes, but none to lose!

Well, the thing was easy—I was a doctor and I had a supply of glycerinated lymph; I had procured some fresh tubes of it only the other day, to hold it up before my audiences while I dilated on its foulness and explained the evils which resulted from its use. Supposing now that I made a few scratches on my arm and rubbed some of this stuff into them, who would be the wiser? The inflammation which would follow would not be sufficient to incapacitate me, and nobody can see through a man's coat sleeve; even if the limb should become swollen or helpless I could pretend that I had strained it. Whatever I had preached to prove my point and forward my ambition, in truth I had never doubted the efficacy of vaccination, although I was well aware of the dangers that might result from the use of impure or contaminated lymph, foul surroundings, and occasionally, perhaps, certain conditions of health in the subject himself. Therefore I had no prejudice to overcome, and certainly I was not a Conscientious Objector.

It came to this then. There were only two reasons why I should not immediately vaccinate myself—first, that I might enjoy in secret a virtuous sense of consistency, which, in the case of a person who had proved himself so remarkably inconsistent in this very matter, would be a mere indulgence of foolish pride; and secondly, because if I did I might be found out. This indeed would be a catastrophe too terrible to think of, but it was not in fact a risk that need be taken into account.

But where was the use of weighing all these pros and cons? Such foolish doubts and idle arguments melted into nothingness before the presence of the spectre that stood upon my threshold, the hideous, spotted Pestilence who had slain my father, who held my daughter by the throat, and who threatened to grip me with his frightful fingers. What were inconsistencies and risks to me compared to my living terror of the Thing that had dominated my whole existence, reappearing at its every crisis, and by some strange fate even when it was far from me, throwing its spell over my mind and fortunes till, because of it, I turned my skill and knowledge to the propagation of a lie, so mischievous in its results that had the world known me as I was it would have done wisely to deal by me as it deals with a dangerous lunatic?

I would do it and at once.

First, although it was unnecessary as all the servants had gone to rest, I locked that door of my study which opened into the hall. The other door I did not think of locking, for beyond it was nothing but the private staircase which led to the wing of the house occupied by Jane and myself. Then I took off my coat and rolled up my shirt sleeve, fastening it with a safety-pin to the linen upon my shoulder. After this I lit a spirit-lamp and sterilised my lancet by heating it in the flame. Now, having provided myself with an ivory point and unsealed the tiny tube of lymph, I sat down in a chair so that the light from the electric lamp fell full upon my arm, and proceeded to scape the skin with the lancet until blood appeared in four or five separate places. Next I took the ivory point, and, after cleansing it, I charged it with the lymph and applied it to the abrasions, being careful to give each of them a liberal dose. The operation finished, I sat still awhile letting my arm hang over the back of the chair, in order that the blood might dry thoroughly before I drew down my shirt sleeve.

It was while I was sitting thus that I heard some movement behind me, and turned round suddenly to find myself face to face with my daughter Jane. She was clothed only in her nightdress and a bedroom wrapper, and stood near to the open staircase door, resting her hand upon the end of a lounge as though to support herself.

For one moment only I saw her and noted the look of horror in her eyes, the next I had touched the switch of the electric light, and, save for the faint blue glimmer of the spirit lamp, there was darkness.

"Father," she said, and in the gloom her voice sounded far away and hollow, "what are you doing to your arm?"

"I stumbled and fell against the corner of the mantelpiece and scratched it," I began wildly, but she stopped me.

"O father, have pity, for I cannot bear to hear you speak what is not true, and—I saw it all."

Then followed a silence made more dreadful by the darkness which the one ghostly point of light seemed to accentuate.

Presently my daughter spoke again.

"Have you no word of comfort to me before I go? How is it that you who have prevented thousands from doing this very thing yet do it yourself secretly and at the dead of night? If you think it safer to vaccinate yourself, why was I, your child, left unvaccinated, and taught that it is a wicked superstition? Father, father, for God's sake, answer me, or I shall go mad."

Then I spoke, as men will speak at the Judgment Day—if there is one—and for the same reason, because I must. "Sit down, Jane, and listen, and, if you do not mind, let it remain dark; I can tell you best in the dark."

Then, briefly, but with clearness and keeping nothing back, I told her all, I—her father—laying every pitiable weakness of my nature open to my child's sight; yes, even to the terror of infection that drove me to the act. All this while Jane answered no word, but when at length I finished she said:—

"My poor father, O my poor father! Why did you not tell me all this years ago, when you could have confessed your mistake? Well, it is done, and you were not to blame in the beginning, for they forced you to it. And now I have come to tell you that I am very ill—that is why I am here—my back aches dreadfully, and I fear that I must have caught this horrible smallpox. Oh! had I known the truth a fortnight ago, I should have let Ernest vaccinate me. It broke my heart to refuse him the first thing he ever asked of me. But I thought of what you would feel and what a disgrace it would be to you. And now—you see.

"Turn up the light, for I must go back. I daresay that we shall never meet again, for remember you are not to come into my room. I will not allow you to come into my room, if I have to kill myself to prevent it. No, you must not kiss me either; I daresay that I have begun to be infectious. Good-bye, father, till we meet again somewhere else, for I am sure that we do not altogether die. Oh! now that I know everything, I should have been glad enough to leave this life—if only I had never—met Ernest," and turning, Jane, my daughter, crept away, gliding up the broad oak stairs back to the room which she was never to quit alive.

As for me, daylight found me still seated in the study, my brain tormented with an agony of remorse and shame which few have lived to feel, and my heart frozen with fear of what the morrow should bring forth.

After but one day of doubt, Jane's sickness proved to be smallpox of the prevailing virulent type. But she was not removed to the hospital, for I kept the thing secret and hired a nurse, who had recently been revaccinated, for her from a London institution. The doctoring I directed myself, although I did not actually see her, not now from any fear of consequences, for I was so utterly miserable that I should have been glad to die even of smallpox, but because she would not suffer it, and because also, had I done so, I might have carried infection far and wide, and should have been liable to prosecution under our isolation laws.

I wished to give up the fight for the seat, but when I suggested it, saying that I was ill, my committee turned upon me fiercely.

"Smallpox," they declared, "was breaking out all over the city, and I should stop there to 'sweep out my own grate,' even if they had to keep me by force. If I did not, they would expose me in a fashion I should not like."

Then I gave in, feeling that after all it did not matter much, as in any case it was impossible for me to leave Dunchester. Personally I had no longer any fear of contagion, for within a week from that fatal night four large vesicles had formed on my arm, and their presence assured me that I was safe. At any other time this knowledge would have rejoiced me more than I can tell, but now, as I have said, I did not greatly care.

Another six days went by, bringing me to the eve of the election. At lunch time I managed to get home, and was rejoiced to find that Jane, who for the past forty-eight hours had been hovering between life and death, had taken a decided turn for the better. Indeed, she told me so herself in quite a strong voice as I stood in the doorway of her room, adding that she hoped I should have a good meeting that night.

It would seem, however, that almost immediately after I left a change for the worse set in, of such a character that Jane felt within herself her last hour was at hand. Then it was that she ordered the nurse to write a telegram at her dictation. It was to Dr. Merchison, and ran: "Come and see me at once, do not delay as I am dying.—Jane."

Within half an hour he was at her door. Then she bade the nurse to throw a sheet over her, so that he might not see her features which were horribly disfigured, and to admit him.

"Listen," she said, speaking through the sheet, "I am dying of the smallpox, and I have sent for you to beg your pardon. I know now that you were right and I was wrong, although it broke my heart to learn it."

Then by slow degrees and in broken words she told him enough of what she had learned to enable him to guess the rest, never dreaming, poor child, of the use to which he would put his knowledge, being too ill indeed to consider the possibilities of a future in which she could have no part.

The rest of that scene has nothing to do with the world; it has nothing to do with me; it is a private matter between two people who are dead, Ernest Merchison and my daughter, Jane Therne. Although my own beliefs are nebulous, and at times non-existent, this was not so in my daughter's case. Nor was it so in the case of Ernest Merchison, who was a Scotchman, with strong religious views which, I understand, under these dreadful circumstances proved comfortable to both of them. At the least, they spoke with confidence of a future meeting, which, if their faith is well founded, was not long delayed indeed; for, strong as he seemed to be, within the year Merchison followed his lover to the churchyard, where they lie side by side.

About half-past six Jane became unconscious, and an hour afterwards she died.

Then in his agony and the bitterness of his just rage a dreadful purpose arose in the mind of Merchison. He went home, changed his clothes, disinfected himself, and afterwards came on to the Agricultural Hall, where I was addressing a mass meeting of the electors. It was a vast and somewhat stormy meeting, for men's minds were terrified and overshadowed by the cases of disease which were reported in ever-increasing numbers, and even the best of my supporters had begun to speculate whether or no my anti-vaccination views were after all so absolutely irrefutable.

Still, my speech, which by design did not touch on the smallpox scare, was received with respect, if not with enthusiasm. I ended it, however, with an eloquent peroration, wherein I begged the people of Dunchester to stand fast by those great principles of individual freedom, which for twenty years it had been my pride and privilege to inculcate; and on the morrow, in spite of all arguments that might be used to dissuade them, fearlessly to give their suffrages to one who for two decades had proved himself to be their friend and the protector of their rights.

I sat down, and when the cheers, with which were mixed a few hoots, had subsided, my chairman asked if any one in the meeting wished to question the candidate.

"I do," said a voice speaking from beneath the shadow of the gallery far away. "I wish to ask Dr. Therne whether he believes in vaccination?"

When the meeting understood the meaning of this jester's question, a titter of laughter swept over it like a ripple over the face of a pond. The chairman, also rising with a smile, said: "Really, I do not think it necessary to put that query to my friend here, seeing that for nearly twenty years he has been recognised throughout England as one of the champions of the anti-vaccination cause which he helped to lead to triumph."

"I repeat the question," said the distant voice again, a cold deep voice with a note in it that to my ears sounded like the knell of approaching doom.

The chairman looked puzzled, then replied: "If my friend will come up here instead of hiding down there in the dark I have no doubt that Dr. Therne will be able to satisfy his curiosity."

There was a little commotion beneath the gallery, and presently a man was seen forcing his way up the length of the huge and crowded hall. For some reason or other the audience watched his slow approach without impatience. A spirit of wonder seemed to have taken possession of them; it was almost as though by some process of telepathy the thought which animated the mind of this questioner had taken a hold of their minds, although they did not quite know what that thought might be. Moreover the sword of smallpox hung over the city, and therefore the subject was of supreme interest. When Death is near, whatever they may pretend, men think of little else.

Now he was at the foot of the platform, and now in the gaunt, powerful frame I recognised my daughter's suitor, Ernest Merchison, and knew that something dreadful was at hand, what I could not guess.

There was still time—I might have pretended to be ill, but my brain was so weary with work and sorrow, and so occupied, what was left of it, in trying to fathom Merchison's meaning, that I let the precious moment slip. At length he was standing close by me, and to me his face was like the face of an avenging angel, and his eyes shone like that angel's sword.

"I wish to ask you, sir," he said again, "whether or no you believe that vaccination is a prophylactic against smallpox."

Once more there were opportunities of escape. I might for instance have asked for a definition of vaccination, of prophylactics and of smallpox, and thus have argued till the audience grew weary. But some God of vengeance fought upon his side, the hand of doom was over me, and a power I could not resist dragged the answer from my lips.

"I think, sir," I replied, "that, as the chairman has told you, the whole of my public record is an answer to your question. I have often expressed my views upon this matter; I see no reason to change them."

Ernest Merchison turned to the audience.

"Men of Dunchester," he said in such trumpet-like and thrilling tones that every face of the multitude gathered there was turned upon him, "Dr. Therne in answer to my questions refers to his well-known views, and says that he has found no reason to change them. His views are that vaccination is useless and even mischievous, and by preaching them he has prevented thousands from being vaccinated. Now I ask him to illustrate his faith by baring his left arm before you all."

What followed? I know not. From the audience went up a great gasp mingled with cries of "yes" and "shame" and "show him." My supporters on the platform murmured in indignation, and I, round whom the whole earth seemed to rush, by an effort recovering my self-control, rose and said:—

"I am here to answer any question, but I ask you to protect me from insult."

Again the tumult and confusion swelled, but through it all, calm as death, inexorable as fate, Ernest Merchison stood at my side. When it had died down, he said:—

"I repeat my challenge. There is smallpox in this city—people are lying dead of it—and many have protected themselves by vaccination: let Dr. Therne prove that he has not done this also by baring his left arm before you all."

The chairman looked at my face and his jaw dropped. "I declare this meeting closed," he said, and I turned to hurry from the platform, whereat there went up a shout of "No, no." It sank to a sudden silence, and again the man with the face of fate spoke.

"Murderer of your own child, I reveal that which you hide!"

Then with his right hand suddenly he caught me by the throat, with his left hand he gripped my linen and my garments, and at one wrench ripped them from my body, leaving my left breast and shoulder naked. And there, patent on the arm where every eye might read them, were those proofs of my infamy which he had sought.

I swooned away, and, as I sank into oblivion, there leapt from the lips of the thousands I had betrayed that awful roar of scorn and fury which has hunted me from my home and still haunts me far across the seas.

My story is done. There is nothing more to tell.

H. Rider Haggard – A Short Biography

Sir Henry Rider Haggard, KBE was born on June 22nd, 1856 at Bradenham in Norfolk, England.

More familiarly known as H. Rider Haggard, he was the eighth of ten children born to Sir William Meybohm Rider Haggard, a barrister (born, incidentally, in St Petersburg, Russia), and Ella Doveton, an author, poet and daughter of a merchant in the East India Trading Company.

Haggard was initially schooled at Garsington Rectory in Oxfordshire where he studied under the tutelage of Reverend H. J. Graham. His elder brothers, who seemed to find more favour with their father, graduated from various private schools whilst Haggard was sent to Ipswich Grammar School, saving his father a considerable sum in fees.

He failed his army entrance exam, and was therefore sent to a private crammer in London in preparation for the entrance exam to the British Foreign Office, which he appears never to have sat. However, it was during his two years in London that Haggard came into contact with a circle of people interested in the study of psychical phenomena and for which he too now developed a life-long interest together with a series of enduring friendships.

In 1875, Haggard's father used his family's connections to send him to Southern Africa to take up an unpaid position as assistant to the secretary to Sir Henry Bulwer, Lieutenant-Governor of the Colony of Natal. In 1876 he was transferred to the staff of Sir Theophilus Shepstone, Special Commissioner for the Transvaal. It was in this role that Haggard was present in Pretoria in April 1877 for the official announcement of the British annexation of the Boer Republic of the Transvaal. The official who had been nominated to read out the Proclamation lost his voice and Haggard was his replacement. It was a moment in history.

Haggard was to remain in the country for six years, during which time he served as Master of the High Court of the Transvaal and an adjutant of the Pretoria Horse.

It was here that he fell in love with Mary Elizabeth "Lilly" Jackson. He hoped to marry her once he obtained more certainty in his career path.

In 1878 he became Registrar of the High Court in the Transvaal and now the time seemed opportune to write to his father to tell him of his hope to marry. The reply from his father was uncompromising. He forbade it until his son had made a proper career for himself.

The following year, 1879, Lily married Frank Archer, a well-to-do banker.

Haggard returned briefly to England to marry a friend of his sister's, Marianna Louisa Margitson, a 21 year old, in 1880, and the couple travelled to Africa together. Haggard's years in Africa had proved, at least on a writing level, rich and inspirational for him, and while still in Natal he wrote two articles for The Gentleman's Magazine describing his experiences.

Moving back to England in (and accounts here differ as to whether it was 1881 or 1882) the couple settled in Ditchingham, Norfolk, Louisa's ancestral home. Later they moved to Kessingland and established connections with the church in Bungay, Suffolk. The marriage produced four children. A son named Jack (who tragically died at age 10 of measles) and three daughters, Angela, Dorothy and Lilias. (Lilias grew to become an author and her father's biographer.)

In England Law was to be the fulcrum of his career. However, although he studied, writing was growing in its appeal to him. His first book, Cetywayo and His White Neighbours, was an account and study of Britain's policies in South Africa.

From this point his career as a writer began to take substantial hold and with it a dramatic shift to fiction. Two years later he published his first fiction, Dawn followed in 1885 by arguably his most popular novel, King Solomon's Mines—detailing the life of the adventurer Allan Quatermain. This was followed the following year, 1886, by She: A History of Adventure, which introduced the female character Ayesha. Both characters, Quatermain and Ayesha, developed a series of books about their adventures.

The study of Law now fell away entirely. He appeared also to have a keen sense of his commercial appreciation. Rather than sell the copyright of his first best-seller, King Solomon's Mines, for a £100 fee he, instead, accepted a 10% royalty. This book is also generally accepted as the first of the Lost World writing genre.

Haggard obviously thought there were many further adventures to tell and it would be hard to find a publisher who would disagree given the start he had made. Sequels soon followed. Allan Quatermain continued his epic and swash-buckling adventures in Africa whilst the sequel to She entitled Ayesha played out her adventures in Tibet. Interestingly Haggard would later extend his characters adventures around the world with Eric Brighteyes, being the basis for an epic Viking romance.

The Haggard family lived at 69 Gunterstone Road in Hammersmith, London, from mid-1885 to mid-1888. It was here that he wrote his most famous works. His time in Africa had given him the experience and atmosphere as well as several observations and friendships of the people who would so influence his fictional characters. Chief among them were the larger-than-life adventurers Frederick Selous and Frederick Russell Burnham. Both were men of Empire and huge ambition as they helped uncover the great mineral wealth of Africa, as well as the ruins of ancient lost civilisations of the continent, such as Great Zimbabwe.

Three of Haggard's books, The Wizard (1896), Black Heart and White Heart; a Zulu Idyll (1896), and Elissa; the Doom of Zimbabwe (1898), are dedicated to Burnham's daughter Nada, the first white child born in Bulawayo; she had been named after Haggard's 1892 book Nada the Lily.

As is typical of the writing of the time his novels contain many of the stereotypes associated with colonialism, yet they also sympathise, to a degree, with the native populations. Africans often play heroic roles in the novels, although the protagonists are more often than not European. The time around the turn of the century was, after all, the great sprint to Empire by many European countries intent on gaining possessions of land, people and resources.

Three of Haggard's novels were written in collaboration with his friend Andrew Lang who shared his interest in the spiritual realm and paranormal phenomena and who was also a greatly admired editor.

Haggard's stories are still widely read today. Ayesha, the female protagonist of She, has been cited as a prototype by psychoanalysts such as Sigmund Freud (in The Interpretation of Dreams) and Carl Jung. Her epithet is, of course, "She Who Must Be Obeyed" and has for decades been used tongue-in-cheek to describe the presumed balance of influence between the sexes.

As a legacy it is easy to establish Haggard, and his pioneering work, as the author of the Lost World branch of writing and its influence of such other writers as Edgar Rice Burroughs, Robert E. Howard and Talbot Mundy. The Allan Quatermain character influenced many 'serials' in Hollywood during the 30s & 40s and can readily be seen as a template for Indiana Jones, the American archaeologist and explorer and huge box office film character.

Years later, when Haggard was a successful novelist, he was contacted by his former love, Lilly Archer, née Jackson. Lily had been deserted by her husband, who had embezzled funds and fled bankrupt to Africa. Haggard installed her and her sons in a house and saw to the children's education. Lilly eventually followed her husband to Africa, where he infected her with syphilis before dying of it himself. Lilly returned to England in late 1907, where Haggard again supported her until her death on April 22nd, 1909.

Haggard also wrote about agricultural and social reform, in part inspired by his experiences in Africa, but also based on what he saw in Europe. By the end of his life, he was adamantly opposed to Bolshevism, a position that he shared with his life-long friend Rudyard Kipling. The two had found friendship upon Kipling's arrival at London in 1889 largely on the strength of their shared opinions.

Haggard was extremely interested in the social affairs of the Country and eager to play a more active part in attempting reform. In 1895 he stood unsuccessfully for Parliament as a Conservative candidate for the Eastern division of Norfolk losing by 198 votes.

Also in 1895 he served on a government commission to examine Salvation Army labour colonies. This, and his heavy involvement in agriculture reform, led to him being a member of several further commissions on land use and related affairs, work that involved several trips to the Colonies and Dominions. This work, in part, helped lead to the passage of the 1909 Development Bill.

In 1911 he served on the Royal Commission examining coastal erosion.

He was an absorbed and dedicated writer of letters to The Times, nearly one hundred were published by them and the bibliography attached below reveals much in the range of subjects he wished to bring attention to.

He was made a Knight Bachelor in 1912 and a Knight Commander of the Order of the British Empire in 1919. Haggard was a member of several clubs including the Athenaeum, Savile, and Authors' clubs.

The district of Rider in British Columbia, Canada, was named in his honour.

Henry Rider Haggard died on May 14th, 1925 at the age of 68. His ashes were buried at Ditchingham Church. His papers are held at the Norfolk Record Office.

The first chapter of his book People of the Mist (1894) is credited with inspiring the 1912 motto of the Royal Air Force (formerly the Royal Flying Corps), Per ardua ad astra. "Through adversity to the stars" (or alternately "Through struggle to the stars") it is also used by other Commonwealth air forces such as the RAAF, RCAF, RNZAF, and the SAAF.

H. Rider Haggard – A Concise Bibliography

Novels
Dawn (1884) Published in three volumes
The Witch's Head (1884) Published in three volumes
King Solomon's Mines (1885) Allan Quatermain series

She: A History of Adventure (1886) Ayesha series
Allan Quatermain (1887) Allan Quatermain series
Jess (1887)
A Tale of Three Lions (1887) Allan Quatermain series
Maiwa's Revenge, or the War of the Little Hand (1888) Allan Quatermain series
Colonel Quaritch, VC (1889) Published in three volumes
Cleopatra (1889)
Beatrice (1890)
The World's Desire (1890) Co-written with Andrew Lang
Eric Brighteyes (1891)
Nada the Lily (1892)
An Heroic Effort (1893)
Montezuma's Daughter (1893)
The People of the Mist (1894)
Heart of the World (1895)
Joan Haste (1895)
The Wizard (1896)
Doctor Therne (1898)
Swallow: A Tale of the Great Trek (1899)
Lysbeth (1901)
Pearl Maiden (1903)
Stella Fregelius: A Tale of Three Destinies (1903)
The Brethren (1904)
Ayesha: The Return of She (1905) Ayesha series
The Way of the Spirit (1906)
Benita (1906)
Fair Margaret (1907)
The Ghost Kings(1908)
The Yellow God (1908)
The Lady of Blossholme (1909)
Morning Star (1910)
Queen Sheba's Ring (1910)
Red Eve (1911)
The Mahatma and the Hare (1911)
Marie (1912) Allan Quatermain series
Child of Storm (1913) Allan Quatermain series
The Wanderer's Necklace (1914)
The Holy Flower (1915) Allan Quatermain series
The Ivory Child (1916) Allan Quatermain series
Finished (1917) Allan Quatermain series]
Love Eternal (1918)
Moon of Israel (1918)
When the World Shook (1919)
The Ancient Allan (1920) Allan Quatermain series
She and Allan (1921) Allan Quatermain series / Ayesha series
The Virgin of the Sun (1922)
Wisdom's Daughter (1923) Ayesha series
Heu-Heu (1924) Allan Quatermain series]

Queen of the Dawn (1925)
The Treasure of the Lake (1926) Allan Quatermain series
Allan and the Ice-Gods (1927) Allan Quatermain series
Mary of Marion Isle (1929)
Belshazzar (1930)

Short Story Collections
Allan's Wife and Other Tales (1889)
Black Heart and White Heart: A Zulu Idyll (1900)
Smith and the Pharaohs (1920)

Publications in Periodicals and Newspapers
A Zulu War-Dance (July 1877) The Gentleman's Magazine
A Visit to the Chief (September 1877) The Gentleman's Magazine
Hydrophobia (letter) (3 November 1885) The Times
The Land Question (letter) (28 April 1886) The Times
About Fiction (February 1887) The Contemporary Review
Mr Rider Haggard and His Critics (letter) (27 April 1887) The Times
Our Position in Cyprus (July 1887) The Contemporary Review
American Copyright (letter) (11 October 1887) The Times
On Going Back (November 1887) Longman's Magazine
Delagoa Bay (letter) (17 December 1887) The Times
South African Policy (letter) (27 December 1887) The Times
Suggested Prologue to a Dramatised Version of She (March 1888) Longman's Magazine
Mr. Meeson's Will (18 June 1888) The Illustrated London News
The Wreck of the Copeland (18 August 1888) The Illustrated London News
Cleopatra (3 December 1888) The Illustrated London News
Hydrophobia and Muzzling (letter) (25 October 1889) The Times
The Annals of Natal (23 November 1889) The Saturday Review
Mummy at St Mary/Woolnoth's (letter) (25 December 1889) The Times
Mummies (letter) (27 December 1889) The Times
The Fate of Swaziland (January 1890) The New Review
In Memoriam (17 May 1890) Thompson's Seasons
American Copyright (letter) (5 June 1890) The Times
Mr Herbert Ward and Mr Stanley (10 November 1890) The Times
Nada the Lily (2 January 1892) The Illustrated London News
A New Argument Against Creation (19 December 1892) The Times
My First Book. Dawn. By H. Rider Haggard (April 1893) The Idler
The Tale of Isandlwana and Rorke's Drift (4 October 1893) The True Story Book
Lobengula (letter) (19 October 1893) The Times
The New Sentiment (letter) (6 November 1893) The Times
Wanted—Imagination   (25 December 1893) The Times
The Fate of Captain Patterson's Party (28 December 1893) The Times
The Three Volume Novel (letter) (27 July 1894) The Times
The Adventures of John Gladwyn Jebb (letter) (30 October 1894) The Times
Agriculture in Norfolk (letter) (30 October 1894) The Times

The Nelson Bazaar (letter) (16 February 1895) The Times
Everything is Peaceful (letter) (20 March 1895) The Times
Lord Kimberley in Norfolk (letter) (17 April 1895) The Times
The East Norfolk Election (letter) (23 July 1895) The Times
The East Norfolk Election (letter) (29 July 1895) The Times
Wilson's Last Fight (7 October 1895) The True Story Book
The Crisis in the Transvaal (letter) (2 January 1896) The Times
The Transvaal Crisis (letter) (13 January 1896) The Times
Jameson's Surrender (letter) (14 March 1896) The Times
The Rinderpest in South Africa (letter) (5 November 1896) The Times
Mr Rider Haggard and Dr Neufeld (letter) (9 January 1899) The Times
Shrinkage of Population in Agricultural Districts (letter) (9 May 1899) The Times
The South African Crisis—An Appeal (letter) (1 July 1899) The Times
Commandant-General Joubert and Mr H Rider Haggard (letter) (8 September 1899) The Times
Anglo-African Writers' Club (17 October 1899) The Times
The War (letter) (25 October 1899) The Times
Farming in 1899 (letter) (22 December 1899) The Times
Farming in 1899 (letter) (1 January 1900) The Times
Settlement of Soldiers in South Africa (letter) (5 May 1900) The Times
1881 and 1900 (letter) (2 October 1900) The Times
Farming in 1900 (letter) (1 January 1901) The Times
Central and Associated Chambers of Agriculture (letter) (6 November 1901) The Times
Small Holdings (letter) (8 November 1901) The Times
Rural England (letter) (4 February 1903) The Times
Mr Rider Haggard on Rural Depopulation (3 May 1903) The Times
Agricultural Distress (letter) (11 June 1903) The Times
The Motor Problem (letter) (24 June 1903) The Times
Fiscal Policy and Agriculture (letter) (16 December 1903) The Times
Telepathy Between a Human Being and a Dog (letter) (21 July 1904) The Times
Telepathy Between a Human Being and a Dog (letter) (9 August 1904) The Times
Mr Rider Haggard on Small Holdings (12 September 1904) The Times
Case L.1139 Dream (October 1904) Journal of the Society for Psychical Research
Mr Rider Haggard on Agriculture (22 October 1904) The Times
Mr Rider Haggard on Rural Housing (27 October 1904) The Times
The Deserted Village (letter) (25 August 1905) The Times
Decrease of Population and the Land (letter) (6 January 1906) The Times
Prevention of Cruelty to Children (3 February 1906) The Times
The New Land and Tenure Bill (letter) (12 March 1906) The Times
Garden City Association (17 March 1906) The Times
Mr H. Rider Haggard on the Zulus (19 May 1906) The Illustrated London News
To Be Proof against British Bullets: A Zulu Incantation (19 May 1906) The Illustrated London News
Housing of the Working Classes (26 June 1906) The Times
Mr Rider Haggard on Small Holdings (4 July 1906) The Times
The Unemployed and Waste City Lands (letter) (19 July 1906) The Times
Mr Rider Haggard on the Transvaal Constitution (7 August 1906) The Times
Vanishing East Anglia (1 September 1906) The Saturday Review
The Land Grabbing at Plaistow (5 September 1906) The Times
The Land Tenure Bill (22 November 1906) The Times

Publishers and the Public (letter) (19 February 1907) The Times
The Careless Children (2 March 1907) The Saturday Review
The Government and the Land (letter) (29 April 1907) The Times
Chambers of Agriculture (2 May 1907) The Times
The Government and the Land (letter) (8 May 1907) The Times
Miss Jebb on Small Holdings (15 June 1907) Country Life
Rural Housing and Sanitation Association (27 June 1907) The Times
St Thomas Hospital Medical School (28 June 1907) The Times
The Land Question (4 July 1907) The Times
A Plea for the Sitting Tennant (letter) (12 August 1907) The Times
A Literary Coincidence (letter) (19 October 1907) The Spectator
Town Planning Conference (26 October 1907) The Times
Dr Barnardo's Homes (16 November 1907) The Times
The Proposed Agricultural Party (5 December 1907) The Times
Mr Rider Haggard and Small Holdings (10 January 1908) The Times
Mr Haggard and Children's Legislation (13 March 1908) The Times
The Drink Trade and Common Sense (letter) (2 April 1908) The Times
The Zulus: The Finest Savage Race in the World (June 1908) The Pall Mall Magazine
Sparrows (letter) (18 August 1908) The Times
Sparrows, Rats and Humanity (letter) (5 September 1908) The Times
The Letters of Queen Victoria (letter) (26 November 1908) The Times
The Romance of the World's Greatest Rivers (December 1908) Travel Magazine
Afforestation. Mr Rider Haggard's View (1 March 1909) The Times
The Late Sir Marshal Clarke (letter) (13 April 1909) The Times
Mr Rider Haggard on Agriculture (27 November 1909) The Times
Mr Rider Haggard on South Africa (11 March 1910) The Times
Why? (letter) (25 April 1910) The Times
Mr Rider Haggard on Irish Agriculture (23 May 1910) The Times
Why Not? (letter) (12 July 1910) The Times
Mr Rider Haggard on Agriculture (16 September 1910) The Times
Mr Rider Haggard on Vermin (8 November 1910) The Times
Danish High Schools (21 December 1910) The Times
Sugar Beet Growing in Norfolk (6 March 1911) The Times
Rural Denmark (letter) (22 March 1911) The Times
Rural Denmark (letter) (3 April 1911) The Times
The Copyright Bill (letter) (6 June 1911) The Times
Mr Rider Haggard on Poverty. The Burden of Civilization (15 July 1911) The Times
Mr Rider Haggard and the Public Records (28 July 1911) The Times
The Farmers' Burden (1 December 1911) The Times
Egyptian Date Farm. The Financial Aspect (11 October 1912) The Times
Umslopogaas and Makokel. Sir H. Rider Haggard on Zulu Types (letter) (16 August 1913) The Times
The Death of Mark Haggard (letter) (10 October 1914) The Times
On the Land. Old Problems and New Ways. The War—and After. (15 March 1915) The Times
Soldiers as Settlers. After-War Problem for the Empire (20 August 1915) The Times
Raids by Air. Zeppelins and Zeppelins (letter) (22 October 1915) The Times
Women's Work on the Land. A Palliative in Hard Times (letter) (29 November 1915) The Times
Women on the Land. Town Girls' Unfitness for Farm Work (letter) (9 December 1915) The Times
Soldiers as Settlers. Sir Rider Haggard's Oversea Mission (2 February 1916) The Times

Soldiers as Settlers (letter) (7 February 1916) The Times
Soldier Settlers. The Future of Rural England (letter) (10 February 1916) The Times
Farewell Luncheon to Sir Rider Haggard (March 1916) United Empire
Soldier Settlers for the Empire. Offer from Victoria (18 April 1916) The Times
Sir R Haggard's Tour. Land for Ex-Service Men (22 July 1916) The Times
Sir H. Rider Haggard's Mission. Land for Ex-Soldiers (1 August 1916) The Times
Land for Ex-Soldiers. Outline of Sir R. Haggard's Report   (12 August 1916) The Times
Empire Land Settlement Deputation to the Secretary of State for the Colonies and the President of the
Board of Agriculture (September 1916) United Empire
Empire Land Settlement by Sir Rider Haggard (December 1916) United Empire
A Journey through Zululand by Sir H Rider Haggard (December 1916) The Windsor Magazine
Mr Wilson's Note. British Publicity (28 December 1916) The Times
Home Produce (letter) (22 February 1917) The Times
The Milk Supply (letter) (11 April 1917) The Times
Corn Production Bill. A National Measure (letter) (13 June 1917) The Times
A Protest and a Plea. Farmers and Meat (letter) (9 October 1917) The Times
Pig-Breeding. A Subject for Municipal Enterprise (letter) (22 February 1918) The Times
The German Colonies. Interests of the Dominions (letter) (5 November 1918) The Times
Light—More Light! (letter) (19 November 1918) The Times
A Great American. Tributes to the Late Mr Roosevelt (letter) (8 January 1919) The Times
Shut the Door (letter) (10 March 1919) The Times
Population and Housing. Emigration v Birth Control (25 March 1919) The Times
The Ex-Kaiser (letter) (11 April 1919) The Times
Empire Birth-Rate. Sir Rider Haggard on Emigration (17 April 1919) The Times
Ex-Service Men Abroad. Warnings from California (letter) (10 May 1919) The Times
Edith Cavell (letter) (16 May 1919) The Times
The Ex-Kaiser. Uncertainties of Trial (letter) (8 July 1919) The Times
Race Suicide Peril. Western Civilization Threatened (11 October 1919) The Times
The British Cinema. Production of Reputable Films (letter) (5 November 1919) The Times
Horrors on the Film. Limits of Publicity (letter) (19 November 1919) The Times
The British Museum (letter) (24 January 1920) The Times
Air Exploration and Empire (letter) (7 February 1920) The Times
The Liberty League. A Campaign Against Bolshevism (letter) (3 March 1920) The Times
Bolshevist Peril. Counter-Propaganda (4 March 1920) The Times
The Empire's Vacant Lands. Settlers and the Food Supply (14 April 1920) The Times
Films and Happy Endings. The Tyranny of a Convention (letter)   (21 April 1921) The Times
Land and its Burdens. Evil of Grinding Taxation (letter) (8 August 1921) The Times
Boy Emigrants (letter) (31 March 1922) The Times
Migration and Morals. Declining Birther Rate (7 April 1922) The Times
Labour Party's Programme. Confiscation and Class Hatred (letter) (28 October 1922) The Times
Efficient Denmark. Keeping the People on the Land (7 December 1922) The Times
The Egyptian Find. Tombs of Eighteenth Dynasty Queens (letter) (19 December 1922) The Times
King Tutankhamen. Reburial in Great Pyramid (letter) (13 February 1923) The Times
The Norfolk Dispute. A Truce while There is Time (letter) (3 April 1923) The Times
Rural Post and Telephone. Minister's Reply to Deputation (19 April 1923) The Times
Liberalism and Land Reform (letter) (1 May 1923) The Times
Small Holdings. Influence of Heredity (letter) (4 July 1923) The Times
Agricultural Parcel Post (26 July 1923) The Times

Country Houses for Sale. Empty East Anglian Mansions (letter) (14 June 1924) The Times
Plight of Agriculture (24 July 1924) The Times
Loans From the British Museum (letter) (30 July 1924) The Times
Zinovieff Letter. Mr MacDonald and a Political Plot (letter) (29 October 1924) The Times
Two Centuries of Publishing. Tributes to Messrs. Longmans (6 November 1924) The Times
Imagination and War (26 November 1924) The Times

Non-Fiction

Cetywayo and His White Neighbours (1882)
A Farmer's Year (1899)
The Last Boer War (1899)
A Winter Pilgrimage (1901)
Rural England (1902)
A Gardener's Year (1905)
The Poor and the Land (1905)
Regeneration (1910)
Rural Denmark (1911)
The Days of My Life (1926)

Film Adaptations

King Solomon's Mines

This novel has been adapted at least six times. The first version, King Solomon's Mines, directed by Robert Stevenson, premiered in 1937. The best known version premiered in 1950: King Solomon's Mines, directed by Compton Bennett and Andrew Marton, was followed in 1959 by a sequel, Watusi. In 1979 a low-budget version directed by Alvin Rakoff, King Solomon's Treasure, combined both King Solomon's Mines and Allan Quatermain in one story. The 1985 film King Solomon's Mines was a tongue-in-cheek parody of the story, with a 1987 sequel in the same vein, Allan Quatermain and the Lost City of Gold. Around the same time an Australian animated TV film came out, King Solomon's Mines. In 2008 a direct-to-video adaptation, Allan Quatermain and the Temple of Skulls, was released.

She

She has been adapted for the cinema at least ten times, and was one of the earliest films to be made, in 1899 as La Colonne de feu (The Pillar of Fire), by Georges Méliès. A 1911 version starred Marguerite Snow, a British-produced version appeared in 1916, and in 1917 Valeska Suratt appeared in a production for Fox which is lost. In 1925 a silent film of She, starring Betty Blythe, was produced with the active participation of Rider Haggard, who wrote the intertitles. This film combines elements from all the books in the series.

A decade later another cinematic version of the novels was released, featuring Helen Gahagan, Randolph Scott and Nigel Bruce. Unlike the book and the other films, this 1935 version was set in the Arctic, rather than Africa, and depicts the ancient civilisation of the story in an Art Deco style, with music by Max Steiner.

The 1965 film She was produced by Hammer Film Productions; it starred Ursula Andress as Ayesha and John Richardson as her reincarnated love, with Peter Cushing and Bernard Cribbins as other members of the expedition.

In 2001 another adaption was released direct-to-video with Ian Duncan as Leo Vincey, Ophélie Winter as Ayesha and Marie Bäumer as Roxane.

Dawn
The film Dawn was released in 1917, starring Hubert Carter and Annie Esmond.

Jess
This book was filmed in 1912, featuring Marguerite Snow, Florence La Badie and James Cruze, in 1914 with Constance Crawley and Arthur Maude, and in 1917 as Heart and Soul, starring Theda Bara in the title role.

Beatrice
The book was adapted into a 1921 Italian silent drama film called The Stronger Passion, directed by Herbert Brenon and starring Marie Doro and Sandro Salvini.

Swallow
The novel was adapted into a 1922 South African film.

Stella Fregelius
The book was adapted into a 1921 British film, Stella.

Moon of Israel
This novel was the basis of a script by Ladislaus Vajda, for film-director Michael Curtiz in his 1924 Austrian epic known as Die Sklavenkönigin (Queen of the Slaves).